Sketch by Ken Cosgrove

Nancy Hart

REBEL HART

By Edith Morris Hemingway
and Jacqueline Cosgrove Shields

SCHOLASTIC INC.
New York Toronto London Auckland Sydney
Mexico City New Delhi Hong Kong Buenos Aires

Nancy Hart was an actual person who fought with the Moccasin Rangers during the early years of the Civil War and was known to be a Confederate spy. However, many of the events and other characters are products of the authors' imaginations.

ISBN-13: 978-0-545-06911-3
ISBN-10: 0-545-06911-4

12 11 10 9 8 7 6 5 4 3 2 1   8 9 10 11 12 13/0

Printed in the U.S.A.   40

First Scholastic printing, March 2008

Little crow, take
solitary flight
on shining wing
through starless night.
Alone, striving to soar,
you persist
and so endure.

J.C.S. and E.M.H.

Contents

Prologue

Early in the Civil War, Federal troops moved in quickly to occupy the mountainous area of western Virginia along the winding miles of the Baltimore and Ohio Railroad. Just as quickly, though silently, Confederate sympathizers banded together in small groups throughout the region. These were mountain men, who knew the hills, trails, and caves by heart, who could ride at night, attack by surprise, and be gone just as quickly, leaving only the echoing taunt of laughter. The raiders were a legitimate part of the Civil War—a valuable source of horses, supplies, and intelligence for the Southern army. They caused thousands of Federal soldiers to be withheld from the actual battlefield to be used as guards, and, in their own way, they helped the Confederate army extend the war into 1865.

One group, led by Perry Conley, called themselves the Moccasin Rangers because they attacked as a moccasin snake, suddenly and without warning. Nancy Hart, an actual person who was fourteen years old at the start of the Civil War, was a valuable member of the rangers. Her story, that of an ordinary young woman caught in the extraordinary circumstances of the war, is an amazing mixture of fact and folklore, documented through the years by old newspapers and an intriguing Civil War photograph.

Chapter One

Myrtle shouted from outside the door. "Mamaw! Mamaw! Come on down to the bridge. You gotta see the sky. It's beautiful!"

"I'm a comin', child. Hold your horses whilst I get my wrap," scolded Nancy. Young Myrtle was always dragging her out to see some spectacle.

But what a spectacle it was! Nancy, with young Myrtle gripping her hand, moved as quickly as her tired legs could carry her through the crunchy snow toward the clearing where the bridge spanned the river. It seemed all the townspeople of Richwood were there.

"Mamaw, look! It's like a yella' pathway across the sky!"

"Hush up, Myrtle, and watch. You'll never see nothin' like this agin."

The grandmother and the little girl stood on the wooden bridge, gazing in awe at the glittering display overhead. The orange-yellow head of the comet hung in the January sky, trailing a milky white tail across the deepening purple twilight. "'Tis a sign, a bad omen," Nancy murmured. Then placing her hands firmly on Myrtle's shoulders, she turned the child to face her. "Mark this year well, young'un. Nineteen and ten. There's sure to be another war soon. A real bad one."

"Do you mean like the War Between the States when you was a girl, Mamaw?" Myrtle asked as they turned to slowly retrace their steps up the steep road to the house.

"Yes 'um," Nancy nodded her head. "That's what I mean. There's a heap of sadness and grief awaitin' to start. I don't reckon I'll be here to see it."

"You ain't fixin' to pass on anytime soon, are you Mamaw?"

"Can't know, young'un, can't know," Nancy said, tightening her grip on Myrtle's hand.

"Tell me again about the war and how you rode horses and shot with the best of the Moccasin Rangers, Mamaw," Myrtle said, knowing that no matter how many times her grandmother repeated the story, it cheered her to tell it.

"Was back in the summer of eighteen and sixty-one," Nancy began. And in her mind she was a young girl of fourteen again wearing her best calico dress, swinging and whirling to the fiddle music while the caller sang out the moves to the dancers on the crowded floor.

"Swing your partner 'round and 'round..."

* * * * *

Nancy's head was spinning and her heart pounding as strains of fiddle music ended. John Price gripped her elbow to hold her steady while the dance floor cleared.

"Can you stand on your own, Nancy?" He laughed at her, pulling her upright again as she fell against him.

"Course I can," she snapped back. She tossed her head, swinging her long black hair over her shoulder. "Jist because you're goin' off to fight with Jeff Davis ain't no cause for insultin' me."

"Why Nancy Hart, would I insult the prettiest girl in six counties when I'm fixin' to go to war?"

"All the more reason for you to be kind to me," she answered softly. Nancy's cheeks, already pink from the dancing, flushed deeper. "I jist need a breath of fresh air and a swallow of cold cider."

"I'd be honored to get you one," John said. He left her standing by the open door with her sister, Mary. The cool night air wafted through the opening.

"It's hot enough for the Kelleys to roast a pig right in this room," Nancy commented to Mary. She lifted her heavy hair off her neck.

"Well, Nancy, some folks know that you can't dance every dance and not run outa breath."

"Aw, Mary, you're jist jealous cause you're carryin' another child and you can't dance ever' dance!" Nancy laughed as she let another young man pull her back to the circle of dancers just as John returned with two cups of cider. Shaking his head with a resigned smile, he handed one to Mary.

"Quiet! Quiet down now!" Liam Kelley stood by the fireplace hitting the side of a jug with a spoon. The music faded, and laughing voices grew quiet. "The reason for this here gatherin' is to wish well two good neighbors who are marchin' off to protect our rights and fight for the Southern Cause. Will Price, step up here and raise a toast to your brothers. It's your place to do so as your pa's no longer with us."

Will, who was standing with his arm around Mary's shoulders, moved through his neighbors to the front of the fireplace. He took the jug from Liam and raised it in the air. "Here's to two of the best men in Roane County, my brothers, John and James. Fight hard and swift and return unharmed to Flat Fork. I'd be joinin' you myself if it warn't for Mary and the four young'uns!"

"Soon to be five young'uns!" a voice chided out.

"Soon to be five!" Will repeated with a grin. He lifted the jug to his lips and took a swig before passing it on to Liam. As the jug passed among the men, the women sipped cider from their cups. A general cheer rose from all in the room.

The music picked up again, and this time one of the old timers plucked the strings of his dulcimer while Granny Thomas from up the road tapped out the rhythm with the spoons against her knee. Nancy couldn't keep her feet still as she listened to the lively beat of the music.

"How little Margaret can sleep through all this din, I sure don't know," Nancy said to her sister, who was seated beside her on the bench.

Leaning back against the wall, Mary rocked the child gently. "As long as she's cradled and rocked, the noise don't matter to her." Mary looked at her sister. "Nancy? Nan?...What ails you?"

Nancy's mouth was wide open, and she sat stone still, staring straight ahead. Mary followed the direction of Nancy's gaze. A giant of a man stood in the center of the room, shaking John by the hand and slapping James on the back. How could she have missed the arrival of such a man! His presence all but filled the room—so tall was he that he would have had to bend low to pass through the door. So broad was he that his shoulders strained the seams of his deerskin jacket. His wide smile with its straight white teeth would dazzle all who saw him.

With a knowing look, Mary reached out with the back of her hand and tapped Nancy on the chin. "Close your trap or you'll catch some flies. You sure won't catch a man gapin' like that."

Nancy snapped her mouth shut, but kept her gaze on the man. "Who is he, Mary, and where did he come from?" she asked in a whisper.

"Will's sure to know." Mary looked around for Will and beckoned him to come to them.

He leaned low to answer the repeated question. "I've heard tell he's Perry Conley from Calhoun County. They say his brother jist joined the Federal army, but Conley took to the hills with his own band of men to fight for the

Southern Cause. Follows his own rules, they say, strikin' here and there like a moccasin and then hidin' away to the caves in the hills. Calls himself a captain. Probably here recruitin' for fighters." Will moved his hand toward baby Margaret, who clutched her father's finger tightly. He smiled down at his wife and daughter. "Think I'll go and make Captain Conley's acquaintance," he said.

"Conley. Perry Conley," Nancy turned the name over in her mind.

"Now, Nan, don't go gettin' any fanciful ideas," Mary said. "You know you're still a young'un."

"I ain't no younger than you was when you met Will," Nancy said sharply. Then in a low voice, "I ain't never seen such a man."

Mary saw the determined look in Nancy's dark eyes, the stubborn set of her jaw, and shook her head sadly. "Little sister, I know what you're thinkin', but it can't be. Jist let it go."

"I think I'm gonna get me a new dancin' partner," Nancy said as she stood, pushed her hair back over her shoulders, smoothed the front of her dress, and, without shifting her gaze from her objective, started toward the center of the room where Conley stood.

The sudden sound of horses' hooves and then the steady thump of marching feet drew everyone's attention from the party. The musicians hesitated and finally ceased altogether when the guests turned to the noises from the road.

"It's Federal troops!" Mrs. Kelley exclaimed, looking around frantically as if she should hide something or someone. She wrung her hands nervously.

"Calm down, Eliza dear," Liam said, "this is western Virginia. We are still part of the Union even though the rest of Virginia has seceded. We must abide with both sides of this war no matter where our sympathies lie."

"Well, I ain't afraid to speak my sympathies, and I don't care who knows it!" Nancy said defiantly. She flounced toward the door, opening it wide, and shouted as loudly as she could into the darkness, "Hurrah for Jeff Davis!"

A hushed silence fell over the room. The mothers automatically reached for their children, ready to make a hurried departure if necessary. Four shots rang out. Nancy felt the air above her head ripple as a minié ball from a Federal rifle whizzed past and thudded into the thick wooden frame of the door. Nancy, her cheeks flaming red against the pallor of her skin, turned her back scornfully on the Federal troops. Trying to hide the fact that her knees were shaking, she managed to say, "If they can't shoot better'n that, Jeff Davis won't have no trouble lickin' 'em!"

Nancy's father swung the door closed while her mother grabbed her by the shoulders, not sure whether to shake her or hug her. "Nancy Hart, you'll be the death of me yet!"

"Or the death of us all," her father joined in. "What are you playin' at, girl?"

Nancy heard her parents, but did not look at them. All the while they were talking, her eyes darted around the room, hoping to see the tall man in the deerskin jacket. But he was not there. *Here I go a riskin' my life and he didn't even see,* she thought.

"Nancy! Nancy, do you hear me?" Her mother insisted, "You can't be so quick to act. It's dangerous, do you hear me?"

"Yes, Ma, I hear," Nancy replied.

"Let's have some music here, folks. Lots of vittles left yet," Liam urged the group of friends and neighbors to continue celebrating. But the joy was gone from the gathering. Gradually each family drifted toward the shelter of their own homes.

Chapter Two

Two days later Nancy strode into the farmyard carrying her brother's hand-me-down rifle and two rabbits she had shot. Her thick hair was plaited down her back, and she had tucked the cumbersome skirt of her dress into her belt the best she could to give her legs more freedom when she rode the horse. One of these days she'd get her ma to let her wear trousers. "Wearin' trousers ain't womanly," she mimicked her mother's tiresome voice. "Yeah, and it ain't necessarily womanly to ride horses, chop wood, mend fences, and shoot rabbits," she added as she laid what was meant to be their supper on the ground and propped the rifle against the side of the barn in preparation to skinning the rabbits.

The sound of men's voices drew her attention. She peered around the side of the barn. And there he was again—Captain Conley, looking even more a giant astride his powerful horse, towering above Pa as they conversed. Two other men, strangers, were with him, but even on their horses, they looked dwarfed beside Conley.

Nancy yanked her skirt from her belt and flounced it out around her legs. Her hands were a mess with dirt and

7

dried blood. She thrust them in the nearby watering trough and rubbed them briskly together. The flurry of activity and anticipation had her heart pounding. As she smoothed her hair and fluffed it out around her face, she raced to the corner of the barn and came to an abrupt halt at the turn. Then she took a deep breath and walked primly into the open with eyes downcast, hoping her beauty was impressing Captain Conley. She looked up just in time to see his broad back as he tipped his hat to her pa and rode down the lane with his two companions.

"Oh, blazes!" she muttered under her breath and stamped her foot, causing a small puff of dust to rise. "Pa! Pa!" she called out as she ran to where he stood. "That was Captain Conley! What did he want, Pa?"

"Oh, he's recruitin' for guides hereabouts. Someone who knows Roane County and these parts like the back of his hand. Someone who could give the slip to even the Home Guard."

"But Pa! That's me! I could..."

"Nancy!" Her father spoke sharply, cutting her off in mid-sentence. "Yer play actin' to the Federal troops t'other night was enough. You'll think of no sech thing! Now git that horse took care of and help your ma with supper." He turned and walked away.

Head down, Nancy slowly walked to where she had left the horse. "Come on, Jeremiah. Let's get this saddle off you and get you fed." The horse plodded along behind her toward the fence. Nancy went through the motions of unstrapping the saddle and heaving it over the top rail, all the while her mind in turmoil.

"Blazes, Jeremiah! I know these hills better'n any person in these parts!"

The horse looked at her with dull eyes and nodded his head up and down as if he understood.

"Pa says Captain Conley needs guides," she said as she removed the bridle and, still holding him by the halter, led him to the pasture gate. "Blast it! I'm better at ridin', shootin', and trail blazin' than any man for miles around!"

Jeremiah, eager now for the succulent green grass in the pasture, nodded again and pulled faster toward the gate.

"No need to tramp on me, Jeremiah," Nancy spoke to the horse. "I could get Will to speak for me since Pa won't. He knows how I can handle a horse and a gun!"

Jeremiah let out a final snort and pulled away from Nancy. He leaned down to take a mouthful of the sweet clover grass and then looked her in the eye as he munched.

"Oh, Jeremiah, you ain't even listenin' to me any more than the rest of 'em." Nancy sighed and gave him a last pat on the rump. She went back through the gate, closed and latched it, and, lifting the heavy saddle from the top of the fence, started toward the barn.

Then with a sudden surge of defiance, she threw the saddle to the ground. Dark eyes shimmering with anger, fists on her hips, she said, "It's me Captain Conley needs to help him, whether he knows it or not! Blast and blazes, it's me that *will* help him!" At this tirade, her voice rose so that Jeremiah lifted his head and whinnied as if in agreement with Nancy's decision.

At the first light of dawn, Nancy slipped away to the meadow behind Will's and Mary's house. She stood on the fence and whistled low. The young filly galloped toward her. Tenderly Nancy talked to her, rubbing her cheek against the horse and offering a carrot she had brought with her. Curling her hand into a fist, she placed it in the hollow between the jaw and neck. "Room to spare," she whispered. "It means you're a fast little lady. That's what Will says."

Then, still cajoling, and straddling the top rail of the fence, she swung her leg over the bare back of the horse. Her weight, light as it was, startled the filly at first, and she pranced sideways, bucking slightly. But Nancy leaned low to the horse's head, stroking her neck and mane, and gripping the horse's sides with her knees. "Quiet. Quiet. You remember me. I've ridden you before. Quiet now, little lady," she whispered and crooned in a soft voice.

As the pink light filled the sky, Nancy and the filly moved, tentatively at first, around and around in an ever widening circle. By the time light streaked the floor of the meadow with dazzling gold, they were in a full gallop, moving as one. Nancy's skirt billowed around her bare legs. She felt the wind in her hair and on her face, the taut muscles of the horse against the pressure of her knees, and the thick hair of the animal as she grasped its mane. At one with the horse's power and speed, she was exhilarated, part of the summer wind, as tall as the trees. Slowing to a canter, she laid her head against the animal's neck, murmuring softly into its ear, "Oh, Lady, you sure are a right pretty little lady, ain't you?"

Nancy cooled the filly down with another wide circle around the meadow, this time at a trot slowing to a walk. As she neared the fence, her attention was drawn by a child's voice.

"Aunt Nan! Mama wants you to come in the house!" Climbing over the rail fence, blonde pigtails bouncing, the little girl stopped short in front of her aunt and turned a freckled face upward. "Come on in and git some coffee and what are you doin' out here so early anyways; that's what Mama says," Louise breathed a sigh, satisfied that she had delivered her message.

"Keep your pigtails on, Lou, and step back so's your toes don't get trod on whilst I git down," said Nancy, as she slid off the horse. "Now, help me walk Lady a bit more and then we'll git us some breakfast." She reached for the child's hand.

Together, hand in hand, they walked Lady, enjoying the silence broken only by morning sounds and the soft thudding of hooves in the dewy grass.

"Nancy Hart and Louise Marie Price! Y'all git in here and git some breakfast while the gettin's good!" Mary's impatient voice pierced the pleasant silence.

Nancy looked at Louise and shrugged her shoulders. "Guess we'd best go in," she said. Conspirators now, the little girl imitated Nancy's shoulder shrug and smiled as they climbed back over the fence and walked toward the house. The aromas of coffee brewing and ham sizzling surrounded Nancy and Louise as they entered the farmhouse kitchen. Will sat at the head of the table, holding five-year-old John on his knee and helping him put on his boots.

"I'm surprised Ma let you come so early what with all the vegetables that need puttin' up for next winter. Well, now you're here..." Mary placed baby Margaret in Nancy's arms and turned toward the stove, picked up a thick towel, and removed a pan of hot biscuits from the oven, all in one motion.

"Ma don't exactly know," Nancy replied as she seated herself next to Will. She bounced the fussy baby up and down a few times, kissed the top of her head, and then skillfully spooned in a mouthful of oatmeal before the baby's wavery smile could disappear.

"Mama, I fell!" whined Virginia as she hobbled through the open doorway with a tragic look on her face.

Mary took one look at the basket Virginia held out in front of her. Yellow gooh dripped through the slats to the floor. "Oh, Lord, my eggs!" she exclaimed. "Ginny, what were you thinkin' of?"

At the sound of the anger in her mother's voice, Ginny's face screwed up tightly, and then with her mouth open wide, she began to bawl. "But my knee, Mama. I hurt my knee!" she sobbed.

"Over here, Ginny. Sit down and let's have a look," Will jumped up, displacing Johnny. Now that he had lost his father's attention, Johnny, too, began to wail loudly. Baby Margaret followed the lead of her big brother and also began to howl, the oatmeal dripping down her chin. Only Louise did not cry, but instead held her hands over her ears and rolled her eyes at Nancy.

Ginny limped pitifully to her father, still crying while Mary knelt and dabbed at her daughter's knee with a damp cloth. "No need for all this caterwaulin', Ginny. It's only a skinned knee," she said. "Hush up you young'uns. The only thing broke around here is all our eggs!" But the noise did not stop.

"Quiet all!" Will demanded in a loud voice.

Johnny wiped his nose on the back of his hand and sniffed. Ginny sobbed more softly. And baby Margaret's cries subsided. In the quiet that settled on the room, Will laid a hand on Mary's shoulder and said, "The hens'll still be layin' tomorrow, darlin'." Then, leaning closer to Ginny, he added, "It was nice of you to scramble the eggs, Ginny. But next time wait till they're in the fry pan." Virginia giggled at her father's joke, and Mary smiled at her husband, her mood changed for the better.

Finally, all seated at the table, they ate heartily without much conversation. When Will settled back with his cup of coffee, he turned to Nancy and said, "What did bring you here so early, Nan?"

"I came here to tell y'all somethin'," Nancy began. "Somethin' important."

"What is it, Nan? Have you got a new beau?" Mary asked.

"I said important," Nancy raised her voice.

"Well, don't git huffed. Go ahead and tell."

"I aim to join up with Captain Conley as a guide, and I'm askin' you to speak for me, Will."

Both Mary and Will looked at her in stunned silence until Nancy prompted them, "Well?"

Mary burst out, "You're crazy, Nan! You're a young'un and you're female! What would they want with the likes of you?"

Nancy leaped up from the table, tipping the chair onto the floor. But before she could put her anger into words, Will stood too, setting the chair upright and pressing Nancy down into it. "Hush up now, both of you!" he said. "Mary, you know as well as I do that Nan's worth two men here on the farm. She can work horses like neither of yer brothers could and she's a good hand with a rifle."

"Will's right, I...," Nancy managed to say.

"I said, hush up!" Will spoke again. "You are good, Nan, but I can't speak for you. First of all, yer ma and pa would never call me kin again if I did. And second, I can't go publicly takin' sides in this here war. I got a farm to run and young'uns to raise, and, to be honest, I need you here to help, Nan. Fact is, you're a gal, you ain't got a horse, nor a decent gun."

Nancy stood again, as defiant as ever. "I made up my mind, Will, and I know good and well yer sympathies lie with the Southern Cause. As for a horse, I was hopin' you'd let me have loan of Lady."

Will shook his head. "I can't loan you Lady, Nan. Yer pa would skin me alive. Best stay home. That's my last word."

Mary, with a defeated look on her face, sat still, her hands resting on the small mound of her unborn baby. "They won't let you stay, Nan. When they see a young girl, they'll jist send you packin'."

Nancy shook her head. "They'll take me. I'll show 'em how I know the trails and caves and how I can handle a rifle. If I don't have a horse, I'll go on my own two feet."

Mary, knowing the stubbornness of her sister, raised her hands and let them drop. "What'll I tell Ma and Pa?"

"Don't tell 'em nothin'. They'll find out soon enough." Already Nancy was heading for the door. "I thought I could go with yer blessin', but I reckon not. You'll hear from me; I'll be around now and agin." She looked at them all staring at her, the children as silent as their parents. Without a good-by or even a lift of her hand, Nancy went outside and closed the door. She went directly to the big sweet gum tree where earlier she had left the squirrel rifle and a few necessities bundled into her shawl. Now she tied the shawl with its bundle around her waist, lifted the rifle, and started resolutely down the road. Before she reached the bend, she heard a child's call, and turning, saw Johnny racing after her. She stood and waited for him.

Johnny, out of breath, held out a parcel. "Mama says you'd best take some vittles with you, lest you starve." Then catching his breath, he added, "Aunt Nan, are you really goin' to be a soldier? Can I come, too?"

Nancy knelt so that she was eye level with the child and hugged him to her. "I hope there's no need for soldierin' by the time you're big enough to go, Johnny. Anyhow, yer papa and mama need you to help here on the farm." She kissed him on the forehead, stood, and turned to walk away.

"Bye, Aunt Nan," he called.

Nancy lifted her hand and waved without turning. She did not want him to see the tears in her eyes.

Chapter Three

The sun was high by the time Nancy stopped to eat some of the ham and biscuits Mary had sent with her. She cupped her hands at the mouth of a spring and drank thirstily. All morning she had kept off the road, not wanting to meet anyone who might recognize her and thus question where she was headed. She wanted to be far into Calhoun County by the time Ma and Pa knew she had left. She had taken a little-used path up and over the ridge. The summer heat and the steep climb with her confining skirt had her thinking again and again about Lady and how much more quickly she would have travelled on horseback.

A sudden shot from a rifle, horses' hooves, and men's voices sent her flying for cover behind a rock. For some distance she had been following a rocky ridge thirty feet or so above a road, and now, looking down just beyond the bend, she caught sight of five Federal cavalry soldiers detaining three mountain men. As she watched, the men were forced to toss their weapons to the ground and then to dismount.

"Looks like we got us some raiders here, Sergeant," she could hear the lieutenant say. "Corporal, dismount and confiscate their rifles."

Conley's men, Nancy thought. *They could be Conley's men.* Swiftly, but silently, she left her squirrel rifle behind the rock and moved beyond the point where the men had stopped. Then without giving herself much time to think, she scrambled down the steep bank to the road and ran toward the soldiers from behind, shouting to draw their attention. "Help! Please help me!" She did not have to pretend to be out of breath from a long run. Her heart was already pounding hard from fright and excitement as she stopped in front of the lieutenant. "They've taken them all! Please help!"

"Whoa, miss!" said the surprised lieutenant. "Who's taking what?"

"The Rebel raiders! They're takin' all our stock! Pa sent me for help."

"Where is this?"

"Just up the road yonder, the farm 'round the bend."

"How many are there?" the lieutenant asked.

"About five or six, I reckon."

Then the lieutenant barked out orders. "Corporal, guard these men. The rest of you follow me. We'll get us a whole passel of prisoners today." He wheeled his horse around, and the others followed, thundering down the road.

Nancy stood behind the young corporal when she spoke to him. "Mighty glad I happened to see you soldier boys when we needed y'all."

"Yes, ma'am," the young man answered without turning. He shifted nervously from one foot to the other, but his eyes never left the prisoners. "You can help me, miss, if you'll just get me the rope off my horse over there."

"I'd be much obliged to help you," Nancy replied. Still out of his range of sight, she picked up a flintlock rifle from the ground. Then thrusting the barrel squarely between the corporal's shoulders, she pulled the hammer with a loud click. "Help you," she repeated, "to put that rifle down nice and easy on the ground."

The three prisoners leaped forward immediately, one taking possession of the corporal's gun, shoulder belt and pistol, another of the corporal himself. The third one gave Nancy a wide smile, and Nancy noticed he had strange, whitish blonde hair that gave him an older look, but his face showed him to be not much older than herself. "That was a right nice performance, miss. For awhile there, we didn't know whose side you was on, but we did know there warn't no more raiders down the road!" He grinned again.

"Save the sweet talk fer later, Josh," the older stocky man said. "We best be outa here afore those soldiers return." As he spoke, he held his knife up to the wide-eyed corporal's throat as if to threaten him, but then with a laugh and a quick motion downwards, he sliced the buttons off his jacket. Josh, with a practiced hand, caught the cascade of brass buttons as they fell.

Retrieving the heavy flintlock rifle from Nancy, the third man thrust the corporal's smaller carbine into her hands. And then, almost in unison, all three were on their horses, Josh holding the reins of the corporal's horse as Nancy climbed up and slid her new-found rifle into its socket on the saddle. She looked over her shoulder to see the young corporal standing in the middle of the road, jacket and mouth agape. Her laughter goaded the soldier into action. He ran down the road in the direction his comrades had gone, his jacket flapping out behind him.

The other two men were off, and Josh looked to Nancy and asked, "Can you handle a horse?" With a disdainful look, Nancy spurred the horse in the direction the others had taken, leaving Josh to be the one to catch up. They left the road immediately, crashing through underbrush. At first it took all Nancy's concentration to keep the two men in sight ahead of her as well as to gain the feel of this new horse. Her feet did not even reach the stirrups, and he was so much bigger and more powerful than Lady. But she could tell he had been trained well. *Here she was,* Nancy thought, *in a matter of minutes with both a horse and a decent rifle, the two things Will had said she lacked. Right nice for jist a gal!*

Now the two men ahead of her branched off, one taking a turn to the right off the trail, the other keeping to the left. Nancy slowed in a moment of uncertainty. Until now she had simply followed, but what was she expected to do? She wasn't even sure they were Conley's men. As if in answer to her unspoken question, Josh drew up next to her.

"Can't stop yet," he said. "Follow me."

"But where are we goin'? Are you with Captain Conley? Can you take me to his camp?"

"You're just full of questions, ain't you, miss...miss?"

"Nancy Hart is my name."

"And I'm Josh Douglas."

"Well, Josh, can you take me to Captain Conley?"

He smiled and nodded. Then pulling ahead of her, he left the path and urged his horse straight up a steep, gravelly slope. Nancy's horse preferred the gentle path, and it took a good deal of her strength and coaxing words to get him to follow Josh. It seemed to her that they travelled in circles, but always moving higher. "The Federals can't follow us here," she called out to Josh. "They ain't smart enough."

He raised his hand in answer and pulled up to wait for her.

"How much farther to Captain Conley? Where are the other two men? Are you all part of Conley's Moccasin Rangers?"

Josh removed his hat. The summer heat had plastered his whitish hair flat against his forehead. He pushed his hair back with his hand. "You talk too much, Nancy Hart. We ain't much fer answerin' questions."

"All right, Josh, but jist one more question. Why the buttons? Do you melt 'em down or collect 'em?"

He laughed out loud. "Is that jist one question?"

When Nancy squirmed impatiently, and the big black gelding stepped sideways, snorting, Josh replied, "A hundred Yankee buttons buys us a brand new rifle from General Wise. That's why. He's gettin' a right good collection of brass buttons."

Satisfied to have at least one of her questions answered, Nancy rode along in silence. They couldn't have gone farther than a few miles when without warning, the older, stocky man joined them. He and Josh merely nodded to each other and continued on. Shortly, from the other direction, Nancy heard sounds of underbrush and twigs breaking. She turned her horse and pulled the carbine from its socket. Lifting the gun, she aimed toward the sound.

"Whoa there, missy. We all know how quick you are with a gun," said the older man.

At the same time Josh leaned forward and reached out to lower Nancy's rifle. Then the third man rode into view, saying, "A fine greetin' that is, to nearly shoot my head off!"

"Aw, Nathaniel, nobody got hurt," Josh spoke up.

The older man looked to Nancy then and tipped his hat. "Luke's the name, miss."

"I'm Nancy Hart."

"Much obliged to you, Miss Nancy. You came along at the right time back there. Have you a place you're headed?" he asked.

"She wants Captain Conley, Luke," Josh answered for her.

"Captain Conley," he repeated, raising his eyebrows. "And what would you be wantin' with Captain Conley?"

"I aim to be his guide for Roane County," Nancy answered decisively.

"His guide, hmmm?" Luke said with a chuckle. "Are you sure you're big enough to find Roane County itself, never mind findin' the trails?" All three of the men laughed at that.

Nancy's face flushed with color. She leaned forward and spoke in a lowered tone. "I had no trouble findin' the three of you this mornin', did I?"

Nathaniel looked to the ground in embarrassment, and Josh muttered, "She's right enough there."

Luke cleared his throat and said, "Well, the decision'll be up to the captain, but I reckon we can at least trust her with his whereabouts. What d'you say, boys?" Josh and Nathaniel nodded in agreement.

Not much farther they left the path again, slowing their horses to pick their way very carefully through the dense growth so as not to form a well-worn track. Finally, they entered a clearing at the base of some high boulders. A woman bent over a small campfire, and two men stood talking together outside a tent. None seemed surprised that the four of them had suddenly emerged from the trees, and Nancy realized that this must be their camp. She scanned the boulders and could see numerous small overhangs and passageways and one large dark entry into the rocks. Now Luke dismounted, and the woman, who appeared older than Nancy first thought, walked to him. She placed a hand on his arm at the same time nodding toward Nancy with raised eyebrows. Nancy gave her a tentative smile, but the woman's frowning look did not change.

"Howdy, Alice," Josh said. "How's my best gal? Got anythin' good simmerin' in that pot?" Alice gave him a disparaging look and turned back to Luke.

"Where's the captain?" was all Luke said.

"Did I hear my name?"

Nancy had never heard his voice, but she knew before she turned toward the sound that it was Conley who had spoken. At that moment he ducked out through the dark hole in the rocks, then straightened to his full height, shading his eyes with one hand and holding a steaming cup in his other. He was eye level with her, though Nancy sat a horse at least fifteen hands high. All Nancy could do was stare at his overpowering presence. Everyone else seemed to diminish in stature.

"Captain, this here's Miss Nancy...aw..., what did you say yer family name is, missy?" said Luke.

"Hart." Nancy was surprised to hear her own voice respond, for she was so spellbound by Captain Conley and his deep blue eyes.

"Ah...the little 'hurrah for Jeff Davis' gal from Roane County," Conley replied.

"She aims to guide us through this here war," Luke said with a wink at the captain.

Then Josh spoke up. "We brought her, Captain, 'cause she saved us from a Federal patrol back there."

"Well, well, let's hear the story," said Conley, giving her his wide, dazzling smile. Nancy managed a small smile in return.

Josh led the black horse away as the woman who was called Alice took Nancy to one of the tents. "Here," she thrust a plate of hot beans toward Nancy and pointed toward a stool. "You look like you ain't et in a week. Beans'll do you good."

Nancy could think of nothing but two blue, blue eyes. "Thank you," she said as she spooned the brown mixture into her mouth.

"Now listen here," Alice said, "you're jist a young'un. You shouldn't be here, mixin' in with this here fight. It ain't fer young'uns."

"I'll be fifteen come July. That ain't such a young'un. Anyways, the Federals seen me, and I held a gun to one of 'em. I can't go back. They'll hang me." The warm food tasted good. She felt more like herself. *That's right,* she thought. *I can't go back now even if they want me to.* She stretched her legs out in front of her, and the small stool tilted as she flexed her back muscles. "Guess I'll jist have to stay here with Captain Conley...and the rangers," she said.

Chapter Four

A large washtub had been placed over a wood fire beside the stream. Nancy bent over it, scrubbing trousers and shirts. Her hands were raw from the hot water and lye soap. Strands of hair clung to her sweaty face, and she tried without success to fling them back over her shoulder. Her back ached from the long hours of leaning over the tub.

"Alice," she complained, "I come here intendin' to fight alongside the men, but alls I've done is woman's work—washin', mendin', cookin'. I'm tired of this. I ain't even seen the outside of this camp in two weeks whilst the men are comin' and goin' with their raids. And listen to them now, laughin' and splashin' upstream while we're here cleanin' their clothes!"

"I tried to tell you, girl," Alice replied as she spread still another pair of trousers over a bush to dry. "The men have mighty high opinions of theirselves, and we women are s'posed to be lookin' out fer them. Sides, it don't look like you mind scrubbin' and mendin' the captain's britches too much. You think I ain't seen you makin' cow eyes at him? But mind you, don't go settin' yer bonnet fer that one. He's already got a wife and two young'uns down to Grantsville."

"I ain't settin' my bonnet fer nobody!" Nancy snapped back at Alice as she splashed the trousers back into the steaming water, turned on her heel, and vigorously dried her hands on her apron.

"Watch out there, Nancy. You tryin' to knock me down?" Josh smiled and bent to pick up his hat that was knocked from his head when Nancy collided with him.

"Oh, Josh, it's you. I jist can't stand 'round here doin' these blazin' chores anymore!" Near tears, Nancy spread her hands out in desperation.

"Let's take a walk and cool off," he suggested. He led her through the thick growth of trees to a steep, rocky trail. They left the path and climbed higher and higher, rocks becoming loose underfoot so that they clattered down the mountainside. At last they came to a ledge that jutted out over the side of the mountain. Josh reached out his hand to pull Nancy up the last big stretch.

Out of breath, Nancy took a moment to breathe in the cool air and let the soothing breeze wrap around her. Finally she sighed. "It's beautiful, Josh," she said as she looked over the dense trees below. The camp was hidden in there somewhere. Beyond that the stream threaded its way through the forest, a silken ribbon. It disappeared into the thickness of trees to reappear sparkling, curving, widening into the valley beyond.

"This is my private place," Josh said. "Been comin' here since I was a young'un."

"It's jist...jist...beautiful," Nancy smiled at Josh.

"Ain't never showed it to nobody else," he said.

There seemed to be a lot of activity when Nancy and Josh walked back into camp. A new man, whom Nancy did not recognize, was conferring closely with Captain Conley. They studied a map and spoke in hushed tones, pointing to different locations. Finally, they each pulled their watches from their pockets and synchronized the time before the stranger tipped his hat and mounted his horse.

While Nancy was busy collecting the shirts and trousers from their drying places, she watched the two men. Alice gave Nancy a warning look as if to say, "Don't ask questions, girl. You'll know when the time is right."

It was a few hours later when Josh said, "Nancy, Captain wants to see you."

She was pouring strong coffee into a tin mug held out by one of the men. "That's enough. You're sloppin' over!" He jumped back to avoid the scalding liquid.

Ignoring him, Nancy placed the coffee pot on the ground near the fire. Her heart beat faster as she followed Josh toward the cave. While she walked, she pulled off her apron, balled it up, and tossed it aside. Brushing her skirt and patting her hair in place, she put on her best smile and entered the cave.

"Where's the farm gal?" Conley said without looking up. He and Luke huddled over a rock shelf which served as a table. A lantern cast light on the map spread out before them.

"Here I am, Captain," she responded.

He looked up and spoke. "Now's your chance, young lady, to prove your worth to us. We're making a raid on a Federal train outa Parkersburg tonight. I won't mention the details 'cause the fewer that know the better, but I need an innocent young farm girl and her brother to be driving a heavy farm wagon on the road south tomorrow." Then he smiled. "Can you do that for us?"

Even in the dim light, his dazzling smile made her heart melt and made her forget all the complaints she had voiced that afternoon. "Course I can, Captain," Nancy caught her breath. "Who'll ride with me?"

"Josh Douglas will be your brother." Turning to Luke, Conley said, "They make a good brother and sister, don't you think?"

"Sure do, if Josh'll do somethin' 'bout that light hair of his. The Federals will see that a mile away and remember it."

"Right. Everything in order then." Conley turned back to studying the map.

Nancy stood there not quite sure of what to do next. Luke guided her from the cave. "Git yer mount ready, and take a few vittles."

She felt a surge of energy and excitement. *A raid! I'm goin' to help on a raid! And next time he calls fer me, he'll say, 'Where's that Nancy Hart?'* **not** *'Where's that farm gal?'*

The next few hours were a confused jumble. In the darkness they broke camp and rode quietly in small groups, staying off the main roads. Finally in the early hours of the morning before dawn, Nancy slept briefly in the loft of a barn while she and Josh waited with a wagon ready. She was in a sleepy daze when Josh shook her awake. "They're here, Nan," he whispered. She quickly combed her hair and plaited it in two long braids to look more like an innocent farm girl.

The men worked swiftly and in complete silence. Before she knew it, the wagon had been loaded with long, low boxes of rifles and ammunition. Then a false wooden floor was added over the top, and immediately the men spread a layer of straw and began shoveling foul-smelling manure on top. Nancy took her place on the front seat of the wagon and gathered up the reins of the sturdy farm horses. Almost as an afterthought, Josh bent down and scooped up two handfuls of dirt and rubbed it through his hair, turning the light color to a dull, tangled mess. Then pulling his wide-brimmed hat down hard over his head, he climbed up next to Nancy, slid his carbine between them under the seat, and took the reins.

Finally Luke whispered, "You know the roads, Josh. We'll be shadowin' you the best we can in the woods along the way, but if you run into a patrol, you're on yer own."

Josh and Nancy both nodded, and they were on their way as the first pink of dawn streaked the sky. The wagon lumbered along the road, the horses straining against the heavy load of the double cargo. Nancy was wide awake now, noticing everything around her as the early morning light grew brighter. They passed a house here and there, and one farmer waved to them as he led his cows out of the milking barn. Nancy waved back vigorously, but Josh nudged her. "Don't call no more attention to yerself than you need to," he said. From then on Nancy wondered with each farm they passed, *Were they Southern or Northern sympathizers, friends or enemies?*

Once she looked sideways at Josh and noticed a lanky strand of whitish hair hanging loose beneath his hat. "You missed a piece, Josh," she said as she reached to tuck it back behind his ear.

His face grew red as he mumbled, "Thanks," and gave his hat another hard tug down. "But my name ain't Josh today. We're the Johnson young'uns takin' this load of sow manure south to our uncle along the Charleston Road. My name's Billy and you're Ruth Ann."

"That's fine then, Billy, but why in blazes does our uncle need this here smelly mess? Don't he have animals of his own?"

"Sure he's got a farm, but not a pig farm, and we do."

"Well, brother Billy, I'm gettin' used to this powerful smell. Could be by the time we get where we're goin', I'll be right fond of it."

"Shhhh." Josh held his hand up. "Listen." A whistle of a bobwhite rang through the woods. Josh whistled the same notes in answer.

"You talkin' with the birds now, brother Billy? I think the smell is turnin' yer brain."

Josh smiled. "Them's our rangers in the woods, sister Ruth Ann. Try it."

Nancy whistled a bobwhite call, and sure enough, from the other side of the road, a whistle came in answer.

As noon approached, Josh looked anxiously at the clouds building in the blue sky. "If it rains and the road turns to mud, we'll be mired fer sure with this heavy load. The ruts are deep enough as it is now." He coaxed the horses on faster, but they soon fell back to their slow, labored pace.

"You got some of them vittles you brought along?" Josh asked.

Nancy pulled out the small package of food she had packed. Handing a biscuit to Josh, she watched as he swallowed it in two gulps. "Pass me one of them apples, will you sister Ruth Ann? Ain't you havin' lunch?" he asked.

"Not hungry." Nancy could barely keep her stomach from flipflopping. "Too excited," she said. "I know these parts 'round here. It's Roane County. We'll be seein' more folks on the road now." She pulled her bonnet up on her head and tied the strings tighter. The broad brim protected her face from the hot sun, as well as from observation.

A wagon moved toward them. The road was just wide enough to allow the two to pass. A few minutes later two horsemen, a Federal officer and a civilian, rode past. The civilian tipped his hat to Josh, who nodded in return. The officer passed, looking straight ahead.

By two o'clock a few scattered raindrops fell from the overcast sky. Josh and Nancy barely spoke, they were so consumed with their own thoughts and worries of getting their cargo to the appointed spot. The silence was broken by three loud crow caws. Nancy looked around for the birds, but did not see any. Three more raucous calls came from the opposite side of the road, and Josh sat up straight, gripping the reins more tensely.

"More birdcalls from our friends?" Nancy asked.

Josh nodded. "These are different. This means danger." He slowed the horses and touched the brim of his hat. "Three crow calls twice in a row is a warnin'."

"But, how do they know we understand?" she asked in a lowered voice, sitting straight backed and stiff, her face hidden below the bonnet brim.

"They know we heard. They're watchin'. Did you see me touch the brim of my hat?"

"Was that a signal?" she asked, surprised.

"You go ahead and pull yer bonnet forward by the brim." Nancy did as Josh said, and immediately three crow caws came from the woods on Nancy's side of the wagon. She stiffened even more, and her legs began to tremble. "My stomach feels like a flock of birds was flyin' 'round in there," she said.

Before Josh could answer, they rounded a bend in the road and saw a farm wagon stopped just ahead. A Federal patrol had set up a checkpoint. "Loosen up, you look too stiff," Josh said to Nancy out of the corner of his mouth.

The wagon in front moved on. The sergeant held up his hand, motioning Josh to stop. Two soldiers took the horses by their bridles to hold them still.

"Afternoon," the sergeant greeted Josh.

"Afternoon," he replied.

In order to keep her hands from shaking, Nancy reached into the lunch packet and pulled out an apple. She polished it on the front of her dress.

"No need to ask what's in this wagon, Sarge," one of the soldiers laughed.

"Yeah," replied his companion, "we could smell 'em before we could see 'em."

An officer sat his horse, supervising the patrol. "Get on with the search! We're not here to make jokes," he said as he backed his horse away from the offensive wagon and fished a handkerchief from his pocket to hold over his nose.

"Yes, sir." The sergeant started walking slowly around the wagon, tapping on its sides with the butt of his rifle.

Knock, knock. *It sounded the same.* Nancy listened for the next rap and the next. *If he hits a hollow spot, he'll know it's a false bottom.* She could tell Josh was nervous, too. The sweat from under the brim of his hat caused some dirt to trickle down the side of his face.

Now the sergeant approached the rear of the wagon. Crunch. Nancy bit into her apple and pretended to choke on it. Cough. Cough. The last knock of the rifle butt could not be heard clearly over her choking sounds.

"Looks like your riding mighty low," the sergeant said to Josh. "Wouldn't have a heavier load in there than meets the eye, would you?"

Before Josh could answer, the officer, who had backed his horse even farther and still held the handkerchief to his nose, said impatiently, "Get on with the inspection, Sergeant. Check the inside!"

Out of the corner of her eye Nancy saw a slight movement of Josh's hand toward the gun beneath the seat. Trying to hide the shaking of her own hand, she took another bite of the apple. The sergeant picked up a twig and gingerly stuck it down into the foul-smelling load. Then the fragile stick broke, and the sergeant suddenly found his hand plunged wrist deep into the manure. "Best sow manure in these parts," Nancy said. "It'll even make yer fingers grow!"

With that, the sergeant yanked his hand out and gave her a nasty look.

"Move along, move along." The mounted officer removed the handkerchief from his face just long enough to give the order.

Immediately Josh shook the reins to urge the horses on, and the two men holding their bridles jumped aside. Nancy glanced back to see the sergeant bend down to wipe his hand on the grass in disgust while the other three men laughed.

When the wagon finally lumbered around the next bend and they were out of sight of the checkpoint, Nancy let out a long sigh of relief. She had not realized that she had been holding her breath. "Do you think we'll meet another patrol, Josh?"

Josh shook his head. "Don't think so. Not much more than a few miles to go."

Nancy was feeling exhilarated now. "My heart was a poundin', but you know, I wasn't really skairt, jist excited like I was play actin'. I think we done right good." She was nearly bouncing around on the seat as she spoke.

Josh gripped her firmly by the arm. "Nancy, don't forgit we're Billy and Ruth Ann. This ain't over yet, and this ain't no fancy play. This is fer real."

Nancy fell silent and slumped down on the seat. She did not speak again until Josh turned the wagon onto a narrow, rutted farm lane. Again, he extended his hand, but this time touched her shoulder lightly. "I didn't mean to insult you, sister Ruth Ann," he said with an apologetic smile. "You did the Moccasin Rangers right proud back there."

Nancy finally smiled in return. "We both did the rangers proud. We showed the captain."

Josh pulled off his hat and wiped the sweat from his forehead, smearing a trail of dirt across his face. "Yonder's our shadows," he said as he waved his hat at Luke and Nathaniel.

Nancy leaned forward, excited to see others from the rangers' camp moving about the farmyard. No one spoke as each person was occupied with a task. The wagon had no sooner stopped when someone was unhitching the weary horses. Josh jumped down from the wagon and ran toward the barn. Nancy retrieved the carbine from under the seat and scrambled down to the ground as a fresh team was hitched up. She saw a young man and a woman in a bonnet, similar to the one she wore, climb up on the wagon. The young man turned the horses and headed out the lane. It all was accomplished in less than ten minutes.

Josh reappeared leading two horses. "Mount up," he said.

Nancy climbed up on the horse. "Tell you one thing," she said to Josh, "when we get to where we're goin', I'm gettin' me some britches." Looking closer at Josh, she added, "And you best get yerself some lye soap and water."

They were the last ones left in the farmyard. "Where did they all go so fast?" she asked.

Josh lowered his voice, "We're gonna lay low fer a few days till talk of this blows over. We're headin' for a cave along the Gauley near Summersville by different roads so as not to draw attention."

"Summersville? Why I can get you there quick. Jist follow me." She urged the horse forward, and Josh followed her without question.

Chapter Five

Talk of the raid on the Federal train did blow over quickly. Some of the not so well-known rangers, who were also farmers, slipped back and forth to their homes to catch up on fieldwork and to check on their families. They also listened to talk among neighbors and in the towns, and they read the newspapers. The seizure of the weapons was quickly overshadowed by talk of two battles to the north and east of them at Rich Mountain and then Corrick's Ford. The newspaper reports focused on the death of Confederate General Robert Garnett, the first general to die in the war on July 13, 1861.

Nancy kicked her legs back and forth, enjoying the freedom of the new trousers she wore. The light inside the cave was dim, but she could see Alice laughing at her.

"I declare! A woman in britches and shirt! I believe it suits you, Nan."

"Well, my ma would have 'somethin' to say 'bout it, Alice. But it sure is a freein' feelin'. Perry Conley wants me to guide us across to Gauley Bridge tonight so's he can survey the area, and I sure ain't gettin' no skirt tangled up in the nettles of these hills."

"Oh, so it's 'Perry Conley' now and not 'the Captain.' Better watch out, missy, or you'll be too big for them britches."

"Don't you worry none 'bout me," Nancy spoke over her shoulder as she left the cave, tucking her plaited hair up under her broad-brimmed hat. "I know these hills better'n anybody, and I know where I'm goin'."

"I surely hope you do, Nancy Hart. I surely hope you do," Alice replied softly.

A steady rain late in the afternoon of July 27 darkened the sky early. Now in the dreary dusk, Nancy stood among the tethered horses of the rangers in the shelter of thick hemlocks. Her clothes were soaked, but her sodden wide-brimmed hat at least kept the raindrops off her face.

"Humph," she said. "He thinks all I'm good for is scoutin' and mindin' the horses." Nancy stroked the big black mount. "You and me are pretty good friends by now, Pepper, even if you once was a Yankee horse. And you know well as I do that we could be down there helpin' the captain and General Wise burn that bridge."

She could see the mass of Confederate troops which had already passed through the covered bridge and knew the other rangers were down among them.

"I know you want to be down there, too," Josh had said earlier when he saw the disappointment on her face. "But it's the scout's job to guard the horses so we can make a fast getaway."

Now Nancy said aloud to the horse, "It's jist on account I'm a girl, that's all, Pepper." The horse bent its head to nuzzle her shoulder.

She could smell the acrid odor of smoke and kerosene before she could see the dark cloud billowing out of the bridge. Then sparks of flame licked here and there at the sides of the bridge and through the roof. The running forms of a few men scurried from the dark opening, but the roof was almost fully engulfed when finally she saw a single, tall figure emerge as if in no hurry. He stood silhouetted against the bright light of the flames and removed his hat to wipe his arm across his forehead.

"All right, Pepper," she said with a sigh of relief, "we'll go back to camp soon now."

Almost daily rainfall halted the activities of the Moccasin Rangers. Discouraged, many of the men returned to their farms to try to salvage their crops and harvest what they could. By August 12, Luke, who faithfully kept a record of each day, announced that it had rained for twenty days. The frequent rainfall continued well into September until finally the cooler, dry autumn weather prevailed.

"Gen'ral Bobby Lee is settin' up on Big Sewell Mountain straight over yonder as the crow flies." Josh pointed toward the distant hills.

"Yeah, wouldn't be far if we was crows, but since we ain't, it would take us a fair time to get there," Nancy replied. She sat close to the fire, shaking out her long dark hair, trying to dry it in the meager heat put out by the small flame.

"Cookin' on this here tiny fire is nigh on to impossible," said Alice. "I don't care what the captain says 'bout spottin' a large flame from below. Ain't a body can see anythin' through all these trees, nohow."

Ignoring his wife's complaint, Luke held out his tin mug while Alice filled it with coffee.

"Hear tell Gen'ral Lee's got nigh to 15,000 troops with him, too," he said.

"They're havin' a time with the measles," Alice interjected. "Losin' quite a few each week, I hear."

"Measles! Why, that's a 'fliction for young'uns," Nancy laughed.

"That's true, but when grown men git it, it ain't no joke," Alice frowned at Nancy.

"Well, ol' Bobby Lee won't git sick 'cause I heard tell he has his own personal hen what sleeps under his cot and lays him a fresh egg each mornin'," Josh said.

Everyone laughed at Josh's joke. "I'm serious," he insisted. "It's true, I tell you."

"Oh, Josh, you're funny," Nancy said as she shook her long curtain of hair near the heat once more. "Thinkin' of cuttin' off my hair. It's jist a bother," she said.

"No," Josh said quickly. "It's too pretty to cut off. Dark as a starless night," he added in a low voice.

"More like a crow's wing, Josh," Captain Conley spoke casually in his deep voice as he entered the small glow of the campfire.

Immediately Nancy sat up straight, a deep blush on her face. She had paid no mind to Josh's compliment, but a "crow's wing" suddenly took on new beauty in her mind. She pulled her hair back and straightened it as best she could. Even in the dim light of the fire, she could see Conley's white teeth flash as he spoke, and she imagined his blue eyes flashing.

"I been thinkin'," Conley said as he sat down on the log next to Josh. "I don't like this talk of Pierpont's about western Virginia breakin' off and formin' its own Union state. He's pickin' up too many supporters. And now the Federal troops are holdin' the entire town of Spencer. The Confederates have 'em surrounded, but can't make any headway because of this young, sharp shootin' doctor, name of Poole, who is holed up in the cupola of the courthouse, pickin' off any Reb that comes in sight. Been up there for days.

"Little Nan, Spencer's your territory, ain't it? In Roane County? Think you could find me my own hidey hole 'round there where I could pick off a certain Doctor Poole myself?"

"Yes, Captain! Course I can," Nancy answered before she could actually visualize the cupola of the courthouse and the surrounding lay of the land. Now her mind worked frantically. *The town of Spencer is mostly flat with small, steep hills all around. There's that high spot, wooded with rocks on top off to the south and east. Would it be within range of his rifle? Could I git him up there? We'd have to leave the horses down below, but there must be enough trees or underbrush to hide in.*

"Good then, Nan. Be ready an hour before dawn. We'll ride out alone. No need for a passel of men and horses to draw attention." Captain Conley stood and stretched his arms far beyond his usual height. "Get a good night's sleep, Nan. We ride early."

Nancy's eyes followed him until the tall figure was swallowed by the darkness, her heart pounding so loudly she was sure the others could hear. Josh lowered his head and stared into the glowing embers of the fire. No one spoke. Finally Alice broke the silence.

"Well, girl, you got yer work cut out fer you. Best get some sleep. Best we all do."

"Yes," Nancy replied, her voice filled with pride and anticipation. "The captain needs me even more now."

Without a word, Josh stood and walked away.

"Now, what's the matter with him?" Nancy asked.

Alice shook her head. "There's none so blind as them that won't see," she said.

Nancy curled herself tightly into her blanket. She closed her eyes, adjusted herself once more on the hard dirt floor of the cave, back pressed against the wall. Sleep would not come. The gentle sound of the small brook which ran through the back of the cave had always soothed her. Why then was it so bothersome tonight? "Hair like a crow's wing," he had said. *Maybe it's not such a good idea to cut it off.* She ran her hand over her body. *Bosoms nearly as big as my sister Mary's, flat stomach, curved hips—a woman. Hope he don't notice the freckles 'cross my nose and on my hands. Should've rubbed lemon on my skin to bleach 'em as Ma said. Oh blazes, he won't notice nothin' with my hair tucked up under a hat and those mannish trousers and shirt on. What will I say to him all the long way to Spencer? What will he say to me? I wish that blasted brook would stop thunderin' away*... A few hours before dawn, her eyes closed, and she slept a sleep full of dreams.

Now, as it turned out, Captain Conley had hardly spoken at all. He had led the way on his own horse up and down the back wooded trails until they were within five miles of Spencer. They maneuvered their horses around underbrush and tall trees. The sun, still low in the eastern sky, streaked the floor of the forest silver and dappled riders and horses with shimmering light.

Finally the captain slowed his horse until she drew alongside. "What can you tell me about Spencer, Nan?"

"Well, my pa and me done a fair amount of horse tradin' in Spencer. There's a town square with the courthouse facin' it." She gave her best dimpled smile, the one she had practiced while peering into the old cracked looking glass on her ma's dresser.

Not noticing, the captain went on. "Don't need to be on top of him to pick him off. This here rifle will cover lots of distance. I want to be to the east, so the good doctor is looking into the sun, and I can get a clear view with the sun behind me."

"There's a high chimney rock a little to the south and east of town. It'll require a bit of hand climbin' to git up, but it should give you a right good prospect," Nancy said. "As I recall, there's underbrush till you git close to the top."

The captain closed his eyes as if trying to visualize it himself. "I'll have to get him on my first shot. If I have to stop and reload, I'll be a sitting duck."

Nancy nodded.

Suddenly the captain smiled and reached to squeeze her shoulder. "Let's have a look at this so-called good prospect, little Nan. We'll see how good a scout you are."

Nancy, hardly able to breathe with her heart pounding right in her throat, managed to spur Pepper on. Her shoulder seemed to burn from the imprint of his hand, and she couldn't keep from touching the spot where he had touched her. They skirted the edge of town and stayed off the road. Finally, they reached the base of the high rock and dismounted.

"You wait here," he said. "If any Yank shows up, you skedaddle. And if you can't, act as though you never laid eyes on me."

Before she knew it, he had shouldered his heavy rifle with the sliding telescopic sight and hoisted himself up the base of the rock. She watched him until he was out of sight, and then she moved to get a view of the cupola through an opening in the trees.

She could see a lone figure moving about the small rooftop perch. The blue-coated man raised his field glasses to his eyes and turned slowly around, surveying in all directions. She held her breath as he turned to look toward the rock. The captain's words came back to her, "I'll be a sitting duck." She swallowed hard. But now the man put his free hand up as if to shade his eyes from the sun, and then he turned to look out the opposite direction. It seemed an eternity until finally one, loud, clear crack of a rifle shattered the silence, sending a flurry of morning birds into flight. Within seconds, the lone figure slumped over the open side of the cupola, arms and head hanging down, his field glasses swinging on a leather strap around his neck. The clatter of his rifle sliding down the slate roof of the courthouse carried across the clear morning air.

Nancy stood there holding the horses, nervously waiting for the captain to appear. She did not look at the cupola. Somehow her eager anticipation had faded when she saw the lifeless figure, which an instant before had been a breathing man. Now suddenly the captain was just above her, handing down the rifle. She reached up and grabbed it, staggering under the heavy weight, and he slid down the base of the boulder. Then, just as quickly, he took the rifle from her, and they were both up into their saddles and riding off.

"Was he a real doctor, I mean that man back there?" Nancy asked Captain Conley after they were a safe distance from Spencer.

Conley pulled up his horse and reached to grasp Pepper's bridle, halting the large animal and startling Nancy. "Listen to me, Nan. That was no man. That was a varmint, no different than a weasel who sneaks into your hen house at night and sucks the life out of all your eggs." Fixing his blue eyes directly on Nancy's face, he moved his head closer to her. "Them Federalists want to sneak in here and suck away all our rights. There's only one way to take care of them. And **we** done that this morning."

He released Pepper, turned, and rode on ahead of her. Embarrassed that she had questioned him and with her thoughts and feelings in turmoil, Nancy rode the rest of the way back to camp in silence.

By mid-October Nancy was homesick. It had been four long months since she had seen Mary, Will, and the young'uns. She knew this was the season her pa made molasses, and she could almost smell the heavy aroma of the hot, bubbly mixture and taste the sweet drippings over Ma's delicious cornbread. Nancy decided it was time to pay a visit.

"Where you headed, Nan?" Josh asked. He stood holding his broad-brimmed hat in one hand. The breeze lifted his white-blonde hair from his forehead and placed it down again in disarray.

"Back home. My sister Mary's fixin' to have another young'un soon now, and she's sure to need my help. I'll jist ride on down there."

Frowning, Josh asked, "Ride on down where? With Federals swarmin' all over the place, you're gonna ride Pepper with "U.S. Cavalry" stamped on his rump clear as day? Are you crazy?"

"I never thought." Nancy sat on the ground. "How am I gonna get home? I never thought." After a brief silence, Nancy smiled up at him. "Josh...I need your help..."

"This is far as I go, Nan. I'll take Pepper back, and you'll have to walk the rest of the way."

Nancy climbed off the horse, lifted her bundle of belongings, and pulled Pepper's head down toward her face. "You're a good ol' boy, Pepper. You sure are," she crooned and rubbed behind the horse's ear. Pepper nuzzled her shoulder, then shook his head.

"Some people sure do rate attention 'round here," Josh said.

"Thank you, Josh. Take good care of Pepper, and I'll bring back a carrot fer you, too." Laughing, Nancy turned and eagerly started walking the few remaining miles toward the Price farm.

Josh raised his hand. "Take care of yer own self, Nan," he called after her.

Chapter Six

When Nancy approached the familiar territory of Will's farm, she felt a strong sense of coming home. "Hope they'll be glad to see me," she muttered.

But on this brilliant red-gold autumn afternoon of October 19, there seemed to be an unusual amount of traffic on the road past the house. From the woods bordering the farm, she could see Will working outside the barn splitting firewood. Johnny and Virginia carried armfuls of the split wood to stack on the kitchen porch. Their voices and laughter rang out clearly, and she opened her mouth to call to them. But another wagon rumbled along, and the driver stopped to have a few words with Will. Then the sound of horses' hooves announced the approach of a small troop of soldiers.

"Blast and blazes! Look at all them Federals," she whispered as she crouched low. When still more wagons approached from the opposite direction, Nancy settled herself in the niche of the old hickory tree. "When I used to hide up here to git away from chores, I never thought you'd come in so handy," she said as she patted the stout tree trunk. "I'll jist settle here till dark.

Don't want no Federal sympathizers noticin' me slippin' inta Mary's house." She wrapped her shawl tightly around her shoulders to ward off the cool dampness that settled over the late afternoon and waited out the last few hours of daylight.

In the fading light of dusk Nancy saw a form approaching across the field. Before she could distinguish his features, she knew who it was. "Pa," slipped out before she realized she had spoken. She wanted to call to him, but did not dare. Instead, she watched as he opened the door and entered the warm kitchen. Within a half hour he left holding John and Virginia each by the hand. Louise skipped ahead. *Must be spendin' the night with Ma and Pa,* she thought. She waited another fifteen minutes until darkness settled and she could see a lamp glowing in a window.

Nancy ran swiftly across the open space between the woods and the farmhouse. She rapped lightly on the kitchen door. In the past she would have walked right in unannounced, but now, unsure of her welcome, she waited in the shadow of the porch. She could feel the vibration of Will's footsteps as he moved through the house. At last the door opened a crack.

"Who is it?" Will asked. Opening the door a bit wider, he asked again, "Who's there?" A shaft of light from the oil lamp he held streaked across the porch.

"Pssst...Will, it's me...Nancy." She spoke in a low voice from the shadows.

"Nan?...Quick, get in," Will said, stepping back into the kitchen.

Nancy slipped in after him, and Will hastily closed the door and slid the bolt into place. Then he pulled the curtain across the window. His shirt tail hung out, and he stood in his stocking feet.

Before either could speak, Mary's voice from the front bedroom called out, "Will, what is it?"

Immediately Nancy went into the other room where Mary was already pushing her cumbersome body up from the bed and pillows, scattering the sewing she had been working on. "Oh, Nan...is it really you, little sister?" Mary reached out, and they embraced, half laughing, half crying.

"There's a lot more of you now than there was afore," Nancy said as she pulled back and placed her hand on the mound which separated them.

Mary put both hands on Nancy's, and they smiled across at each other. "Feel that?" she said when the baby moved beneath their touch.

"How much longer?" Nancy asked.

"Oh, a few more weeks, I reckon. We'll know when it's time. But, Nancy, what's brought you back home? I been so worried, and we never heard a word from you. All this talk of Conley's Moccasin Rangers and the shootin' of Doctor Poole has folks 'round here all riled up."

"Now Mary, don't **you** go gettin' all riled up again." Will said while he gently pressed Mary back down to the bed, helping her settle against the pile of pillows and bolster behind her.

Nancy gathered up the scattered sewing and put it in the basket. Then she said, "Don't worry, Mary. I'll stay here to help out as long as you need me."

"Nancy," Will said, "you can't jist show up here again. Folks'll get wind that you're back, and things jist ain't the same as they was. It's like a war within a war. Not only the North fightin' the South, but neighbors fightin' neighbors, the Home Guard makin' its own rules. There's this new state ordinance 'bout western Virginia legally separatin' from the rest of Virginia. And then there's the likes of the Moccasin Rangers stirrin' the pot."

"Yeah, Nan," Mary interrupted. "Do you know Pa had a hard time gettin' a fair price fer his crop at market jist on account of folks think Perry Conley shot that Doctor Poole off the courthouse roof, and folks know you're in them hills with the rangers now. Course I know you'd never go along with no shootin' of people..."

Nancy turned her head away from Mary. She could not meet her sister's eyes.

Mary abruptly stopped talking. Then more slowly she asked, "Would you, Nan?..."

When Nancy did not respond, Mary drooped her head forward. In a whisper she said, "Oh, little sister, what have you got yerself inta?"

An awkward silence filled the room. Will leaned forward to put a reassuring hand on Mary's shoulder, while Nancy walked to the small bed in the corner where little Margaret slept soundly. Nancy reached down to run her hand over the soft brown curls and touched the smooth pink cheek. Margaret stirred and sucked noisily on her thumb while Nancy retucked the quilt around her. "Maggie, you're growin' like a weed," she said softly.

Finally Nancy looked at Mary, and she could see by Mary's resigned look that in that short span of time she had accepted, though not approved, the fact of Nancy's involvement.

"Well, Nan, we was jist gettin' settled fer the night when you arrived. You can sleep upstairs in Ginny and Louise's bed since they done gone to Ma and Pa's."

"For tonight," Will interrupted.

"By the way," Mary continued, "you look right fetchin' in them britches, though I don't think Ma would take to them. Better put on yer dress tomorra' afore she sets eyes on you."

Nancy grinned at her older sister and then hugged her. "Thanks, Mary."

"Nan," Will began. She straightened. She did not want to hear what he was about to say. She knew that she would have to leave.

Speaking almost in a whisper now, he said, "You can take Lady..."

Before he could continue, the sound of horses' hooves outside warned of more unexpected visitors. All three stared at each other in surprise, then concern.

"Who could that be now?" Mary asked.

"I'll step outside and take a look," Will said. He looked at Nancy: "Best make yerself scarce."

By now there was a loud knock on the door. Will picked up the small oil lamp and walked slowly toward the front door where a second, more demanding knock pounded. "I'm comin'. I'm comin'. Let a man get his britches on," he called out. "Maybe slip out the back," he whispered to Nancy. Will opened the front door and closed it behind him.

Nancy ran quickly to the kitchen and paused at the door, placing her hand on the bolt. Just before she slipped it back, a horse whinnied outside. *Blazes, they're out back too!* She fairly flew back into the bedroom. The sisters looked at each other for an instant in panic. Nancy crouched down as if to crawl beneath the bed, but Mary whispered, "No, that's the first place they'd look." Then despite the awkwardness of her body, Mary was up and already pulling the batting from the partially finished bolster cover she had been stitching. In another instant the batting was tucked away in the blanket chest, and she was holding the end of the bolster cover open. "In here, Nan," she whispered. "Quick!"

They could hear loud voices outside. "Yes, Colonel," Will said, "I reckon I could speak at the meetin'. But it's late now. I'll come on down in the mornin'."

Mary pulled the bolster cover over Nancy's head. "Get up on the bed. That's right. Now pull your feet in." Nancy curled into a curved position against the headboard of the bed while Mary hastily sewed the opening of the bolster cover with a few wide stitches.

The voices outside continued. "Let me git my boots on and tell my wife I'm goin' with you. I'll be out directly."

Now Mary placed several pillows up against the bolster that hid her sister. Nancy fought the panic that was rising in her. Nearly suffocating from her tight enclosure, she took several gasps for air, then forced herself to breathe calmly and slowly.

As the front door opened, Mary quickly crossed the room, picked up Margaret, and hurriedly settled herself back against the pillows and Nancy. The child set up a howl of protest at being disturbed and wriggled to free herself. Nancy could feel her sister's back tremble against her, though Mary's voice sounded calm enough when she spoke soothingly to Margaret.

Will entered the house, but from the sound of approaching footsteps, he was not alone. "Please wait in the sittin' room, Colonel. My wife's feelin' poorly. She's expectin' at any time now."

Nancy fought another tremor of rising panic. She was so tightly wedged into this position that the cloth pressed against her nose and mouth. *Like bein' in a shroud*—the thought had her suffocating again. She could see nothing, but she could hear everything. Someone entered the room. The door latched closed. Then the reassuring voice of Will, "I'll have to go inta town, Mary. They want me to speak in favor of the new state ordinance at the rally tomorra' mornin'."

Mary spoke in an indignant whisper. "They can't make you speak fer somethin' you don't believe in! We're Virginians!"

"Mary, darlin'," Will spoke back softly, "I have no choice. They're here with their men and their weapons. I have to go in order to protect you and the young'uns and the farm."

Heavy footsteps bounded up the stairs and moved through the room above. Mary's back stiffened against Nancy. "What are they doin' in the girls' room?" she asked, no longer whispering.

Before Will could speak, the door swung open abruptly, banging against the wall. A gruff voice responded, "Lookin', ma'am. We're lookin' for any renegade that might have a reason to come visitin'."

"You have no right to burst in here!" Mary said in outrage. "And you've 'wakened my child." Margaret was now wailing in fright.

"Mary, darlin', don't get riled." Will spoke in his ever calm voice. "Colonel, I'll thank you not to walk in on my wife and my child. I said I'll go with you to speak fer the ordinance, but let a man git his boots and coat."

Disregarding Will's statement, the colonel said, "Men, in here. Check under the bed, all the cupboards and chests, and don't forget the outhouse. Now, ma'am, I have reason to believe that your sister, a Miss Nancy Hart, is living among those bushwhacking murderers of Perry Conley's. When was the last time you had occasion to see her?"

Nancy tried not to tremble. *I gotta be still. I gotta be still.* She could feel Mary's back stiff and hard against her, as if to say, *they'll have to go through me to get to you, little sister.*

"It's been nigh onta four months now, Colonel," Will spoke for her, and Mary crooned to Margaret, rocking back and forth and swaying the bed.

The sounds of cupboard doors slamming open, the sounds of shattering crockery, and the pounding, pounding of boots rang throughout the house as Nancy huddled in the dark, with her eyes closed, jaw set, expecting that at any time she would be torn from her dark hiding place.

The colonel ignored Will's answer. "Come now, Mistress Price. A young girl, barely fifteen years, gone from her family for four months with no contact? I find that hard to believe."

"Colonel, you are upsettin' my wife." Will interrupted. "Can't this conversation be continued outside?"

"Mistress Price," the colonel persisted, "have you spoken with your sister recently?"

"No. We ain't laid eyes on her since the day she left," Mary insisted. "But, Colonel, my husband is needed on the farm. I can't tend the animals and do no heavy work."

"Ma'am, your husband will return after he has spoken in favor of the ordinance for forming the state of West Virginia."

Then Nancy heard a voice she had not heard before. "Colonel Poole, no one else on the premises, sir."

"Are you certain, Sergeant?"

"Yes, sir."

"All right. Wait for us outside."

"I hope you are satisfied now that you got my baby cryin'," Mary spoke up. "It'll take me the best part of the night to get her settled." Nancy was amazed at her sister's cool, icy voice.

But the colonel was not apologetic. Instead he replied, "Listen here, those Moccasin Rangers are nothing but outlaws and criminals. And those who help them are traitors." Abruptly he said to Will, "I'll be outside. You have a few minutes to calm your outspoken wife." He slammed out the front door.

Margaret's cries were now just sighs punctuated with hiccups. Nancy felt Mary lean forward. *I can come out now.*

But Will spoke in a whisper, "Wherever she is, keep her there for awhile. They'll be watchin'." Then in a normal voice he said, "I'll stop by the Hughes' farm and ask Harley to tend the horses in the mornin'. Don't worry, darlin'. I'll be back tomorra' afternoon."

Nancy heard Mary catch her breath and felt her sigh. She could picture Will bending to kiss his wife good-by.

Silence settled over the house for a few minutes before either dared to move or speak. Finally Mary's weight shifted on the bed as she rose cumbersomely, still holding Margaret.

"Mary," Nancy whispered as she wriggled. "Mary," she repeated louder, "for Lord's sake, let me outa this tomb."

"Hush, keep still. It ain't safe yet," Mary answered in a low voice. Nancy could hear her soothing little Margaret. "You settle inta a nice sleep now. Your pa will be back tomorra'."

Nancy listened as Mary slid the bolt into place on the front door. "Mary!" Once more Nancy cried almost in panic.

"Hush up. Jist let me make sure all the window curtains are closed," Mary said.

Nancy willed herself to be still. Presently she felt Mary's hand on her back and heard the snip, snip of the darning scissors clip the wide stitches which closed Nancy into her hiding place.

"Stay still. I don't want to nip you," Mary said as Nancy, feet first, emerged from her cocoon. She filled her lungs with great gulps of fresh air. Then she fell into her sister's arms.

"Who was that man, Mary? The colonel, I mean," Nancy asked. "How can they jist take Will off like that to speak for somethin' he don't believe in?"

"It was Colonel Poole."

"Poole?" Nancy questioned and felt herself pale. "Any relation to the Doctor Poole that Capt...that was killed off the courthouse in Spencer?"

Mary looked Nancy straight in the eye and nodded. "His father, and they say he ain't been the same since he carried his son's body down them steps. He vowed to get even with them rangers. Nancy, it's like Will tried to tell you—a war within a war."

The two women sat together on the bed, comforting each other in silence. Finally Nancy said, "Mary, you should sleep. Don't you worry none. You saw to it yourself that everythin' in the house is locked up tight." Nancy leaned forward and held her hand near the chimney of the oil lamp to blow out the flame.

Mary leaned back wearily upon the bed to rest. "Feels funny not to have that lumpy old pillow at my back." She smiled into the darkness.

"That lumpy old pillow is gonna get some rest her own self," Nancy replied. She left the room and in the darkness felt her way up the stairs into the bedroom above. Instead of crawling into bed as Mary had done, Nancy knelt on the floor and looked through the small dormer window. Her eyes were adjusted to the darkness, and in the pale moonlight outside, she could see the silhouette of a horse and a man standing beside it, rifle propped against his side as he lit his pipe and tossed the spent match away. *Will was right. They've left a guard to make sure I'm not here.* Quietly she tiptoed to the opposite window and, sure enough, another man leaned against the back fence.

Unable to relax in the only real bed she'd seen in four months, Nancy spent the long night, curled on the hard floor next to the window, dozing fitfully. Finally at dawn, she saw the two soldiers mount their horses and ride off down the road in the direction of Spencer. Nancy waited still another hour before she crept downstairs to peek in on the sleeping Mary and Margaret and went into the kitchen to build a fire for breakfast. Then she began to clean up the mess that "them blasted Home Guards" had made the night before.

Chapter Seven

"Mama, why is the door locked? Open up. We got fresh molasses!" Virginia shouted from outside the kitchen door.

Mary placed Margaret on the floor and lumbered to the door. "Hush up, Ginny, or you'll wake the dead," she said as she slid back the bolt.

"What's all the lockin' up about, Mary? Scairt the goblins'll git you?" Her pa entered the kitchen, carrying a bucket of molasses. His smile was replaced by a shocked look as soon as he saw Nancy turn from the stove to face him. Father and daughter comtemplated each other in silence.

"Aunt Nan, Aunt Nan!" Louise was at Nancy's side, jumping up and down. Johnny joined his sister to get a hug from Nancy. "Aunt Nan, will you stay home now, or do you hafta go away agin?" Louise asked.

Not looking at the children, but meeting her father's eyes directly, Nancy replied, "Well, Lou, I guess I'll hafta be agoin' pretty soon now."

Without a word, her father turned and went out the door. Mary followed. "Pa," she said. "Pa, at least talk to her."

"Best lock the door agin, Mary," he replied. Then he turned toward home.

The chatter and noise of the children seemed to fill up the room. After silently watching her father's departure, Nancy allowed herself to be drawn back to the demands of Louise, who clung to her waist, and Johnny, who pulled at her hand. Looking over the heads of the children, the sisters exchanged glances. "Don't worry none, little sister," Mary said. "When Will gits back, he'll talk them around."

"Where's Papa?" Ginny asked, as she placed a basket on the table. "We didn't see him in the barn."

Mary put her arm around Ginny and with a forced smile said, "Your pa's gone inta town to give a speech. He'll be home afore nightfall." Then pulling aside the cloth on the basket, she added, "Mmmm, some of Mamaw's cornbread. We'll have some fer breakfast."

The day dragged on. Mr. Hughes stopped by to feed the horses, and Nancy kept to the upstairs rooms, dusting and doing small chores that Mary could not get to. By mid-afternoon, when Will had still not returned, Nancy changed into her dress, taking the time to add two of Mary's fluffy petticoats, and then combed her hair and pinned it up on top of her head.

"You look right pretty, Aunt Nan," Louise said. "Why you gettin' all primped up? Are you goin' out somewheres tonight?"

"No," Nancy shook her head. "It's jist in case your mamaw and papaw stop by this evenin'. You know your mamaw don't take to women in men's britches."

Still later, as Mary prepared supper, Ginny asked, "Do I set a place for Papa?"

Mary answered, "Yes, of course. He'll be home directly." Her eyes kept returning to the window. "Johnny, you run out to the road and see if you can see your pa comin'."

An hour later, Mary placed a plate of food in the oven. "We'll jist keep it hot for your papa. And young'uns, if the soldiers come back with your papa, it's best not to mention Aunt Nan."

"Why, Mama?" Ginny asked. She had been by her mother's side all day.

"Jist best left unspoken, Ginny. It's a secret."

What if the soldiers come agin? Will I have time to hide? The thought of being confined in that almost airless, dark bolster cover again sent shivers down Nancy's spine.

"Is it like a game, Mama?" Johnny asked. "Like hide and seek?"

"Yes, like hide and seek," Mary said with a smile. But the smile soon faded, and this time Mary herself, wiping her hands on her apron, walked slowly outside to the gate in the twilight to look for Will before the last light was completely gone. She paused at the fence, placed her hands spread wide on her lower back and stretched. Nancy, holding Margaret, watched from behind the sitting room curtains. Head down, Mary turned and walked slowly back to the house.

"Will I still keep his plate hot for him, Mama?" Ginny asked as soon as her mother entered the room.

Mary snapped at her, "Why would you ask me that, child, when I said he'd be home directly!"

Ginny's face crumpled into tears, and Nancy placed a protective arm around her. "Your ma didn't mean it, Ginny. It's jist she's tired out from the baby."

Mary sank wearily into a chair. Taking Margaret in her arms, she rocked back and forth. "I'm sorry, Ginny. I'm sorry. He'll be home directly, is all."

And so the night wore on.

Before daylight Nancy moved silently down the stairs and into the kitchen. Mary was sitting in her rocker in front of the cookstove, now grown cold. She was pale and haggard. "Mary, what are you doin' up so early? Did you sleep at all?"

Mary shook her head and rubbed her hands across her round belly.

"Is it painin' you?" Nancy asked.

"No, no. Jist a bit tight at times like it was pushin' at me to stretch its own feet. You forgit, Nan. This is my fifth. I'll know when it's my time."

Nancy moved swiftly now. She placed a shawl around her sister's shoulders, then bent to build up the fire. "You'll feel better when you git some hot coffee in you."

By the time the children awoke and came to the kitchen, Nancy had the room warm and breakfast prepared. Ginny took charge of Margaret, feeding her cornmeal mush while Nancy kept Johnny and Louise busy. Once Ginny looked up and said, "Mama, where's..." but Nancy flashed her such a stern look of warning that she changed to "...how are you feelin' today?"

"Baby's a kickin' up a fury," Mary said. Then she sat up straighter. "Did you hear that? Is that the gatherin' bell ringin'?"

Both women turned by instinct toward the distant sound of the steadily clanging bell. Nancy pressed Mary back down in her rocker. "It's probably jist old man Jensen catchin' his haystack afire agin. They're callin' the neighbor men together to help. Don't you worry none," she said. Just the same Nancy walked to the sitting room window to have a look outside.

"What is it, Nan? Do you see Will?"

"No, no, Mary, jist rest," Nancy put out her hand as if to hold Mary back because now she could see her pa and Mr. Hughes and the Hughes boy walking slowly, heads down toward the house. And on a lead rope behind young Harley was a horse with something long and limp draped over it. Nancy's heart began to pound and suddenly she was sweating, her hands shaking. *No! No!* she screamed silently in her mind. Aloud she called out, "You young'uns stay here with your mama!" And immediately she was unbolting the door and running out to the lane.

Her pa looked like an old man. He stared long and hard at her, but did not speak.

"Pa, what happened?" she asked in a strangled voice.

"You happened, girl. **You,** goin' off with them bush-whackers brought all this down on our heads! I ain't got but one daughter now, and that's poor Mary."

"But, Pa, I..."

"That's my final word. You ain't my daughter no more."

She heard an anguished scream, and the two older men moved quickly, toward the house and Mary. Nancy stared at the horse with the figure of Will stretched across the saddle facedown, a dried blood stain in the middle of his back. Clutching her fists hard against her stomach, she looked at young Harley and opened her mouth, but the words would not come.

The boy, looking at the ground, mumbled so that Nancy had to lean in close to hear the answer to her unspoken question. "We found him in the woods near our place. Shot in the back with a sign pinned on him. Death to..."

"What did it say?" Nancy managed to ask. She had not heard the last word mumbled by the young boy.

"Traitors," he repeated. "Death to traitors."

"Traitor!" The word rang in her head. *Will? A traitor? Never! No one 'round here would call Will a traitor.*

The large plow horse shifted and pawed at the ground, causing Will's rigid arms to swing from side to side like the pendulum of a clock. In her mind Nancy saw clearly the blue-coated body of Doctor Poole slumped over the side of the cupola, his arms outstretched and the field glasses swinging from side to side. "Colonel Poole! It had to be Colonel Poole after he took Will from here the other night."

Nancy was aware of anguished crying behind her, and she turned to see her pa and Mr. Hughes supporting Mary between them. Tears streamed down Mary's face, and she kept repeating, "Will, Will, Will..." Ginny and Louise clung to their mother's skirt, their wails mingled with hers. Only Johnny stood silently with large dark eyes staring at where Nancy stood. Then slowly, as if in a daze, he walked toward her. When she went to kneel and put her arms around him, he moved right past Nancy and walked to the horse.

"Papa?" he said in a small, questioning voice and reached out to touch a stiff hand. "Papa," he repeated, "wake up." He tugged at the open hand now. "Get up. Get up! What's the matter, Aunt Nan? Why won't Papa answer me?"

"Oh, Johnny, he can't hear you." Then the tears started. A torrent of them flowed from Nancy's eyes, and she reached out blindly to embrace Johnny. "I'll get even with 'im, Johnny. Colonel Poole will not get away with this." She spoke through tears which streamed down her nose and into her mouth and down her neck into the collar of her dress. She could feel Johnny's body shaking with his own sobs. "No Federalist can call your papa a traitor. Will was a good man! A good Southern man!"

And now there were more people around them—a wagonful of neighbor women had arrived, summoned by the gathering bell. They had come to cook food and to take care of the laying out as they always did when a neighbor died. Someone was prying her hands away from Johnny, and other hands were taking Will from the horse.

"Mamaw," Johnny said. "Papa won't waken. I called him and called him, but he won't waken."

Hearing this, Nancy slowly straightened and turned toward her mother. "Ma," she said.

The older woman turned her back on her daughter. Then taking Johnny by the hand, she said, "Hush, child, hush. Come with me now, and we'll see to yer mama."

There were people all around her, but no one spoke to Nancy, nor touched or comforted her. One by one the other neighbor women entered the house, laden with baskets of food. Nancy huddled alone beneath the big sweet gum tree and cried until there were no tears left in her.

Finally, feeling drained and exhausted, she walked to the springhouse. Plunging her hands into the trough of cold-flowing water, she splashed some onto her face; then she used her apron to pat her face and hands dry.

For some time she had been aware of the intermittent sounds of sawing and hammering coming from the barn. Now she headed in that direction. She had always felt more at home with the men at their chores than with the women in the kitchen. She stood just inside the open door, allowing her eyes to adjust to the dim light and breathing in the scent of fresh sawn pine. She watched as the men worked, their backs to her. John Hart and Harley Hughes worked steadily and rhythmically. Sawing a fresh plank to size, Harley passed it to John, who hammered it into place. Nancy could see the long form of a coffin take shape. *Will's coffin.* "It weren't my fault, Pa," she spoke out.

Startled by her voice, he turned, looked at her, then turned his face away.

"Pa, won't you listen to me?" she said louder this time. But the only response was the steady beat of his hammer as he drove the nails home. "Like it or not, you **are** my pa!" Nancy shouted. Head held high, she marched toward the house.

A low murmur of voices and the clatter of dishes mingled with the smells of spices and food bubbling on the stove. Nancy entered the kitchen, and all the voices hushed. The only sound was from the rattling lids of the simmering pots. Even Ginny looked at her accusingly with eyes swollen and red from crying. Nancy instinctively put out her arms, but at the same time Eliza Kelley pulled the girl against her as if she needed protection from her aunt.

"Where's Mary?" Nancy stood in the center of the kitchen. "Shun me if you have a need to, but first you tell me where's my sister." Her voice rose more than she had intended. No one spoke. Nancy pushed her way through the women who stood in front of the doorway to the sitting room. "This here's my sister's place, and it ain't your'n," she glared. Reluctantly, the women stepped aside and returned to their tasks.

The sitting room was silent. The curtains were pulled to cover the windows. In the semi-darkness, Nancy saw the body of Will laid out on a makeshift table made from a door. She held her hand across her mouth, trapping a gasp in mid-throat. It was Will's body, Nancy knew, but at the same time something inside her was shouting, *That's not Will. Will's not stiff and still and yella' lookin'. Will's always movin' and laughin' and carin' 'bout people.*

Unaware of Nancy's presence old Granny Thomas and Nellie Hughes spoke quietly as they worked to dress Will in his suitcoat. "I seen half of this valley inta this world, and I seen many a body out." Granny Thomas shook her head as she hunched over Will, tugging his jacket into place.

"And now with this here war, many more a good man like Will Price'll be leavin' this valley never to come back," Nellie added.

"This war's fixin' to be a widow maker," said Granny.

"Like poor Mary in yonder." Nellie nodded in the direction of the bedroom. "As close as Mary was to her time, it ain't no wonder all that thrashin' about and sobbin' would send her inta birthin'."

"The good Lord no sooner takes one than he sees fit to send another," Granny replied.

"What? You mean Mary has gone inta her birthin' time?" Nancy asked, frantic now to get to her sister.

Both women looked up in surprise. Nancy held her hands up in front of her, expecting to be shunned yet again. Instead, old Granny moved toward her, clasping Nancy's hand warmly between her old gnarled ones. "Best get in the room yonder, child, and help your sister."

Nancy looked for a long moment into Granny's kind, old eyes and nodded. Then, thinking only of Mary and the baby, she rushed to the bedroom door. She flung it open, giving Mary, who was propped against pillows, a direct view of her dead husband. Mary screamed a heart-wrenching, "Will!" The scream turned into a low moan that did not cease.

"Shut that door!" Nancy's mother turned from the side of the bed where she and two other women were attending Mary. "I should've knowed it was you. Ain't you done enough harm?" Then lowering her voice, "Do you want to take her new young'un, too? Go away. Jist go away from us. Leave us be." She shoved Nancy out of the room and closed the door. The wailing cries of Mary's anguish could still be heard.

Nancy felt as if she were freezing and burning up at the same time. She covered her ears to shut out the sound. It did not help.

"She don't mean it, child." Granny had her arms gently around Nancy, leading her toward the front door of the house. "As I see it, you're no more to blame for this grievin' than the rest of us. You can abide yonder to my place for a bit till things quieten here, if you've a mind to."

Nancy found herself alone, sitting under the sweet gum tree. She could not think. She could not feel.

"Aunt Nan." She felt a tug on her sleeve. "Wake up, Aunt Nan." Johnny's voice wavered, ready to cry. "Wake up," he repeated.

"I ain't asleep, Johnny."

"What are you doin'?" Lou stood in front of Nancy, her yellow braids turned dark in the last light of day.

"Jist settin'." She reached out to put her arm around Johnny. Louise knelt next to her aunt and placed her head on Nancy's shoulder. The three sat in silence watching the dusky sky turn into night.

The opening of the door spilled a fan of light across the porch and down the steps. Nancy's mother called out, "Louise, John, you all get in here, now. Come and see yer mama and yer new little brother."

Johnny leaped from Nancy's arm and ran toward the house and the inviting light. "A new brother?" he asked his grandmother as he climbed the steps. "Mama, Mama!" he called entering the house.

"Do you hear, Aunt Nan? A new brother. Come on. Mama will surely want to see you," Louise tugged at Nancy's arm.

"No, Lou. You go and give 'im a hug and kiss from me." She gently let Lou's hand go. The girl hesitated, then turned and ran toward the house and her grandmother. Nancy watched as the two stepped into the house. The door closed, and the light was gone. She sat alone in the darkness.

Chapter Eight

Nancy shivered and hunched down as low as she could to the saddle. It had been a long, cold night and had taken all her concentration to control the skittish Lady, who was unfamiliar with rocky, mountain trails and thick forests, let alone being ridden for miles and miles. "Easy now, Lady, easy," she whispered close to the filly's ear and stroked her neck. "We're almost home now." Nancy could see her breath as she spoke, and her hands were so numb she could scarcely feel the reins. Her feet were like blocks of ice in the stirrups. "You ain't as big and powerful as Pepper, but you sure can turn easy and squeeze inta places he can't fit. You and me'll be a good team, Lady, once you get the hang of it."

Last night Nancy had simply gone to the barn, saddled up Lady, and had ridden off without food, or even so much as a warm wrap. And she had not stolen Lady, she told herself. After all, hadn't Will told her that night, which now seemed so long ago, that she could have Lady?

Now Nancy put her hands to her mouth to imitate a crow's call. "Caw. Caw." The cold morning mist closed around her. Her hair, damp and tangled, clung to her face and the back of her neck.

"Caw. Caw." The signal was returned. Nathaniel stepped out of the thick pines beside the narrow trail. "Nancy, is that you, gal? You look like a skinned rabbit and half froze."

She entered camp, using her last bit of energy to guide the skittish horse. Josh was there, reaching out to help her dismount. Nancy slumped against him, comforted by the sound of his voice, but too weary to listen to the words. Then through a dizzying mist she saw Conley. The captain lifted her in his arms and carried her. Resting her head against his broad chest, Nancy fell into an exhausted sleep before he covered the short distance to the cave.

She was warm. She arched her back and stretched her arms and legs. "Mmmmm, warm," Nancy whispered and opened her eyes.

"Well, you sure did have a fine sleep fer yerself," Alice said to the girl, nearly hidden in the pile of blankets at the back of the cave. A small fire crackled nearby. "Here, sit up and get some of this soup inside of you. Then you can tell me what happened."

Suddenly Nancy remembered. And the weight of grief and loss engulfed her. For a long moment she could not speak. She wanted to curl back up into a little ball and just sleep and sleep and never have to think about anything else.

Finally Alice brought the bowl of thick barley soup to her and said, as she eased Nancy into a sitting position, "You don't hafta talk, child. Jist eat this. Everthin' seems worse when yer hungry."

The aroma of the soup made Nancy aware of the gnawing hunger in her stomach. "I ain't et since yesterday mornin'," she said as she greedily spooned in the thick, dark mixture. It glided easily down her throat, warming her.

"Since the day afore yesterday," Alice corrected as she handed her a thick crust of bread. "You slept all yesterday and all night."

Nancy looked up in surprise, but continued to devour the soup and then used the crust of bread to sop up what was left in the bowl. She popped the crust into her mouth. Her hunger satisfied, she began to talk. The story spilled out as though from a burst dam. It flowed, a torrent of words pulling her down into a dark whirlpool of grief. Nancy did not notice Josh, who sat just inside the cave entrance listening.

"...Then my ma closed the door against me. Oh, Alice, I ain't got no one now." Nancy buried her face in her hands. Her shoulders trembled as she cried.

"You got us, Nancy Hart. Me and Luke and Josh and all the rangers. You never hafta be alone if you don't want to." Alice placed her arm around the girl's shoulder. With her other hand she wiped her own eyes. "Smoke from the fire," she mumbled by way of explanation. "Come on now, day's half gone. Sun's been up more'n two hour. We got work to do." She gave a nod toward Josh, and he got up and left the cave.

Nancy rose from the blankets and stood stretching, her slight frame lost in the voluminous folds of Alice's muslin nightdress. Fingering the neatly folded bundle of her dress and Mary's petticoats which lay nearby, she said, "First thing I gotta do is get me some new britches."

"I'll help you," Alice replied.

The corners of Nancy's mouth lifted in a faint smile. "Thank you," she said softly.

Nancy rested the barrel of her unloaded carbine on a post and carefully lined up a distant tree in the sight. Click. She turned slightly and aimed at a single red leaf wavering on a branch. Click. Next, a squirrel moving unaware across the top of a rock. Click.

"Who you shootin', Nan?"

Nancy jumped. "Oh, it's you, Josh." She turned back to her post and the carbine and lined up another tree in the sight. "A varmint," she said, "I'm shootin' a varmint every time I pull this trigger."

"You don't hafta do it yerself, Nan," Josh said gently. "I'd do it fer you...you know."

Nancy shook her head. "I reckon one real shot this far up in the hills ain't gonna bring no Federals swoopin' down on us," she said as she loaded the carbine and snapped it closed. "See that jug a hangin' from that tree limb yonder?"

As Josh placed his hand to shade his eyes, Nancy aimed and fired. The jug shattered, and fragments flew in all directions.

"You're a fine shot with that carbine, Nan. Mighty glad you're with us and not agin' us," Conley spoke as he approached. "Practicin'? Can you tell me what you're plannin'?" He sat on a boulder so that he was eye level to Nancy.

"I'm amin' to get me a pole cat, is what, Captain." She met his gaze squarely. "And I aim to do my huntin' on my own."

"You've strong feelin's 'bout this, Nan. And you've a right to. But I think you should take along some help on your huntin' expedition."

"Thank you kindly, Captain. But it's a family matter and somethin' I need to tend to by myself."

Conley stood. His blue eyes flashed. "Now listen, Nancy. This here's a war we're in, not a mountain feud. Yer family ain't the only one sufferin'." The captain towered over the girl whose small chin was set defiantly. "You best simmer down and give some time and thinkin' to yer plannin', little Nan. Moccasin Rangers can't afford no mistakes." He turned and strode away.

"Now you got his dander up," Josh said after Conley was out of earshot. "You best wait and we can all go together, like the captain says."

"He didn't say nothin' of the kind," Nancy insisted.

Josh grasped Nancy by the shoulders. His voice rose in anger and frustration. "Let us help, Nan. You can't do everthin' alone!"

"You can help, Josh."

He released his grip on her shoulders as his anger began to subside.

She continued, "What you can do is write a letter for me to Mary after I done it, so's she knows it's takin' care of. You've had more learnin' than me and can write it down." Nancy gave him a smile, tossed her dark hair and left him staring after her as she scrambled down the hill.

A few days later Nancy slid off Lady and tied her to the hitching post. Her hair lay on her shoulders, sparkling blue-black in the morning sunlight. She wore her dress, patched and washed by Alice. Mary's petticoats filled out the skirt so that it floated and swung just above her shoes. A shawl and bonnet completed the picture. She was the perfect, demure farm girl, come to peddle some apples and eggs to the soldiers. Taking a deep breath to compose herself, she walked toward the sentry posted at the gate to the Union encampment on the hill just outside Spencer.

"Mornin', sir," she said with a smile.

"Mornin', ma'am," the young sentry said, pulling himself up straighter and smiling back. He removed his hat in deference to her. "What can I do for you?"

"Well, sir, mister officer," Nancy began.

"I ain't no officer, ma'am."

"You look mighty important to me, sir," Nancy said, still smiling her charming smile. "I have a basket of fresh-laid eggs and some of the sweetest tastin', juiciest apples in Roane County that I thought some of you soldier boys might be wantin' for yer supper tonight. I'd be most obliged to jist give you a apple, sir, but I thought the cook might be wantin' to buy some from me to make the officers a pie." She took one of the shiniest apples from her basket and held it out to him.

"Well, ma'am. They do look mighty tasty." He accepted the apple. "See that big tent up yonder? That there's the cook tent, and you'll find the colonel's cook there. Cook's a bit grumpy, but I'm sure you'll have no trouble."

Following the sentry's directions, Nancy proceeded leisurely through the camp, loosening her bonnet strings and letting the bonnet fall back off her head. She looked from side to side, carefully observing the layout of the camp and also smiling fetchingly at any soldier who looked her way.

Now standing inside the tent, Nancy waited to be noticed. The sides of the tent were rolled up, front and back flaps open, but still the air was full of the smells of fat burning, coffee boiling, and steam rising into the air from simmering pots over the fire.

"Clear the way, clear the way there!" A wooden paddle was thrust into the far opening of the tent, supporting several loaves of fragrant, newly baked bread. Grasping the long paddle were two hands as big as hams, which belonged to an enormous man. Nancy had never seen anyone so fat. "Clear the way, hot bread here." He plopped the bread down on a table and placed the paddle upright on the ground, grasping the handle. "Well, what's yer business?"

"Are you the cook, please?" Nancy asked.

Wiping his hands on the apron which stretched across his huge belly, he moved closer to her. His massive face cracked into a crooked toothed smile. "I am the cook to one and all that you see in this here camp, miss. And it ain't no easy job at that. Now what can I do fer you?"

"I have some fresh eggs and ripe apples that my ma says will make a sweet pie fer the colonel. Would you like to buy them?"

He reached out a hand, engulfing the basket handle. "Let's see here. Eggs look fresh, and yer ma's right. The colonel does like a nice apple tart now and then. I'll give you a dollar for it all." He went to the table, opened a drawer, and removed a coin box.

"Won't the apple tarts get cold by the time they get to the colonel's tent?" Nancy asked, wide eyed, as though that were the most natural question in the world.

"Naw, why see up there on that little hill where ol' glory is wavin'? That's the colonel's tent. We just cover his dinner with a towel, and it's run right up to him, pipin' hot." He dropped the coin into Nancy's hand, obviously proud of his pipin' hot food.

"Oh, I see," she smiled sweetly. "That's Colonel Johnson's tent up there, then?"

The large man laughed so that his eyes disappeared into creases of fat and his heavy jowls quivered in his pink face. "Naw, you got all mixed up. Colonel Johnson's troop is over to Calhoun County. This here's Colonel Poole."

Nancy put her head down. "Well, ain't I foolish. Don't know one officer from t'other."

"That's all right, little miss. When you got more apples and eggs, you come on back," he said as he handed her the empty basket.

Oh, I'll come on back sooner than you expect, Nancy said to herself.

During the next week, Nancy and Lady covered the two hour distance from the rangers' cave hideout to the Federal encampment at various times of the day, scouting out the different vantage points from the surrounding wooded areas. She was dressed once again as a boy in britches, wool jacket, and broad-brimmed hat, hoping she would not be recognized in passing as the pretty young farm girl. Careful to stay within the protection of the forest, she surveyed the camp from different angles, always keeping the flag and the tent atop the small hill in view. "Nice of Colonel Poole to put a flag at his front door, ain't it, Lady?"

Finally on a dismal rainy day, she saw him. He was shouting orders, and she couldn't mistake that voice anywhere. The last time she had heard it was when she was hidden in that suffocating pillowcase. Now that she was sure what Colonel Poole looked like, with his dark muttonchops and highfalutin uniform, she patted Lady's neck and said, "Soon as it stops rainin', we'll come a callin' agin."

Early one clear morning, Nancy rode toward the Federal encampment and heard the bugle call and drumbeat of reveille. She knew her spot. "Easy, Lady," she whispered, "you've been here afore. It's jist like we practiced." She held the horse steady with pressure from her knees and leaned in against a tree. The Federal flag lifted in the slight morning breeze. Puffs of smoke rose from small campfires as men prepared their morning coffee. Nancy lifted the carbine, sighted down the barrel, and waited.

Her tense fingers began to grow tired. Her knees ached from the pressure of holding herself steady on Lady. *Maybe the colonel's already up and outa his tent or could be he spent last night at his house in town.* Lady snorted and pawed the ground restlessly. "Quiet, Lady, we'll be movin' soon enough."

The flap of the tent moved, and Nancy stiffened. Her heart began to race, and her throat grew dry. The flap was thrown back. Colonel Poole, with his ugly sideburns and dressed in shirtsleeves and trousers, bent through the opening. He straightened himself to his full stature. One red suspender drooped around his hip. The other stretched over his shoulder. Then, as if taking a look around at the day, he turned facing directly toward Nancy. He opened his mouth in a wide yawn, and reached his arms above his head in an early morning stretch.

Nancy took one hard swallow. *This is fer you, Will.* And she pulled the trigger. The loud crack of the carbine filled the air. Lady jumped nervously, and Nancy nearly dropped the gun. She grabbed the reins to control Lady and quickly looked back at the camp. Men were shouting and looking wildly around. Others were emerging from their tents. Colonel Poole, a red stain spreading across his chest to mingle with the red suspender, clung to the flagpole outside his tent and slowly slid to the ground.

Nancy wheeled Lady around and quickly guided her deeper into the woods. She did not feel the instant thrill of triumph that she had expected, or even a sense of relief. She felt only a dull sickness, and then fear swept through her. She couldn't head toward the cave. Lady's hoofprints in the soft, wet earth would lead them straight to the Moccasin Rangers' hideout! *Blazes, I knowed I should've waited till the ground dried out.* She urged Lady up a steep, gravelly slope where the hoofprints would not show, but Lady stumbled and nearly went down.

When they reached the top of the ridge, Nancy dismounted. "Rest a bit, Lady. I'm gonna have me a look." She looped the reins around a low branch and cautiously approached the rocky ledge. Lying on her stomach, she peered over the edge. There they were below—mounted soldiers following her. *Blazes! They got 'em a tracker. Wide-brimmed hat and a deerskin jacket ain't no Federal army uniform.* The man knelt, looked at the ground, then pointed in her direction. She froze. It was as though he were looking right at her.

The officer in command shouted orders. The mounted soldiers spread out and began slowly moving upward. Nancy, afraid to stand, wriggled backward into the cover of trees. Frantic now, she thought, *What can I do? What can I do?* Forcing herself to calm down, she thought again, *What would the captain do?* And the answer was simple. Find a stream, and hide her tracks in the streambed.

She raced Lady, crashing through underbrush and swerving around trees to the remembered stream. From years back in her childhood she remembered that waterfall with the little hole carved out behind. It couldn't be too far from here. As she rode, she prayed, *Please, please, let there be enough water flowing to hide me and Lady behind it. With all the rain we had, there's gotta be enough!*

When they reached the stream, Lady shied away and would not enter the cold, fast-flowing water. Nancy slid off and stepped in, knee deep. It was cold, so cold, but she couldn't think of that now. She pulled Lady after her by the reins. "This ain't no time to go dainty on me, Lady. I should've brought Pepper. He ain't skairt of no cold water."

The girl and the horse followed the streambed always upwards, slipping and stumbling on the flat rocks. From farther upstream, she could hear the louder rush of the remembered waterfall, but she resisted the temptation to go onto the bank in order to make faster progress. *Can't leave tracks,* she told herself. Finally, out of breath and soaked to the waist, Nancy reached the pool at the base of a twenty-foot cliff. The water fell in a thick curtain from the ledge above, sparkling rainbows in the sunlight and splashing into the pool below. Nancy plunged in farther, pulling Lady. The filly stood her ground, water swirling around her legs, her eyes wide with fear, her nostrils flared, and her ears flattened back against her head.

Nancy put her mouth close to the horse's ear so she could be heard above the sound of falling water. "Easy, Lady, easy," she whispered as she stroked her mane. "You can do it. All we gotta do is step through that water to the hole behind. Come on, girl, come on..." One step at a time they moved forward, Nancy always coaxing. She stiffened at the shock of icy water that fell over her head and shoulders. Finally, they passed through the roaring, splashing, frigid curtain up onto the hollowed rock ledge beyond. Lady tossed her head and shook off the water as a dog does when it is wet. Nancy wished she could do the same. There was no room for her to stand without clinging to the horse, so instead she climbed back onto Lady, crouching down low to keep from bumping her head. She pulled off her sopping wet hat and, with her cheek resting against Lady's neck, she released her plait of hair. Her black hair spread across her shoulders and mingled with the horse's mane. She was so cold, shivering uncontrollably, and her feet were numb. Very slowly she began to feel the warmth from Lady's body creep into hers, but still she shook.

In the misty, semi-darkness a small, red spot appeared in the center of the waterfall. It grew rapidly, spreading until the entire waterfall glared blood red. *No!* A voice screamed inside her. Nancy jerked her head upward and opened her eyes. *A dream. Jist a dream,* she told herself. *I wonder how long I been asleep.*

Now Lady shifted and moved her head as if sensing something. Sounds could barely be heard above the constant rush of the water. And then Nancy saw them— shadowy forms moving across the stream in the light beyond the curtain of water. She gasped and held her breath, at the same time tightening her grip on Lady's bridle to check any movement of the horse. The wavery forms on horseback moved across the stream two or three at a time just a few feet away from where she hid. Now one figure, closer, stopped, and the horse bent its head down to drink. It was the tracker. Nancy could tell by the wide-brimmed hat. The man looked around. Nancy forced herself to breathe. Slowly she reached down to the socket on the side of her saddle and was reassured by the solid feel of her carbine.

If I can see him, can he see me? No, she answered herself. *They got the sun shinin' on them and on the waterfall. I got the dark in here.*

The tracker's horse lifted its head, satisfied, but the rider lingered, still looking toward her. Nancy reached down once more, this time pulling the carbine slowly and gently from its socket. Grateful that she had reloaded the gun earlier, Nancy raised it into position. At last the man turned his horse and started back the way he had come. She watched as the others passed by, following the tracker. Still Nancy held the carbine. It was a long time until she slid the gun back into the socket.

Hours passed. Nancy was careful not to fall asleep again. She told herself she had to stay on guard until nightfall. Finally, when the waterfall shone like liquid silver in the moonlight, the girl and horse ventured out, and travelled, wet and shivering, under the cloak of darkness.

Chapter Nine

Once again Nancy was hunched low and chilled to the bone when at last she reached the cave hideout. She was worried about Lady. The horse's breathing had a harsh rasping sound, and she had moved slower and slower as the night progressed. It wasn't as Nancy had planned. She had seen herself returning in broad daylight, sitting proud and tall on Lady, having accomplished what she set out to do. And the captain would be there to meet her with a broad grin on his face. He would lift her lightly from the saddle and say what a good job she had done and would want her always by his side.

Instead, most of the rangers were gone and the captain was nowhere to be seen. Josh was the one who pulled her, sodden and exhausted, from the saddle. Without speaking, Luke immediately started rubbing Lady down from head to flank with a heavy blanket. Josh wrapped another blanket tightly around Nancy's shoulders and prodded her toward Pepper, who was saddled up and waiting.

"Where is everybody, Josh?" she asked.

"No time to rest and ask questions, Nan. Them Federals have been combin' these hills fer the best part of the day and half the night. Everybody's scattered. Only Luke and me's been waitin' fer you."

"Alice?" she asked.

"Even Alice done gone back to her place. Luke wouldn't listen to no argument from her. Here, drink this. Sorry it ain't nothin' hot, but it'll help you." He held out a jug to Nancy.

She raised it to her lips and took a gulp as she had seen her pa do. The burning corn liquor raced down her throat. She coughed and sputtered as its warmth began to spread through her, driving away the chill. She wrapped the blanket closer around her. Nothing was the way it was supposed to be. "I got my varmint, Josh," she said.

Josh stopped long enough to look directly into her eyes and said, "I knowed you would, Nan. You always do what you set out to do." He gave her a brief smile and then bent to hoist her up onto Pepper's back. "You're tired, but we gotta keep movin'. Alice is expectin' us afore daybreak."

Luke was already sitting on his horse with Lady tied to a lead behind him. Single file they travelled through what remained of the night, winding down the mountainside through the thick growth of trees. The bright moon shone above the screen of tree branches, scattering patches of pale light on the little caravan. Nancy began to think that all she ever did was ride, cold and shivering, through dark woods along rocky trails. The only solace now was that she was no longer alone. Luke was in front of her leading the way with Lady trudging wearily along. And close behind Nancy was Josh. It was good to know that at any time she could look back to see him, tireless, sitting straight in the saddle, hair sleek and silvery in the moonlight.

Pepper's steady gait, plodding slowly and rhythmically, rocked Nancy into near sleep. Her head bent forward; she jerked it up quickly and opened her eyes at the sound of Josh's voice.

"Stay awake, Nan. Not much farther now." On the widening trail, he had pulled his horse up next to her and reached out to grasp her arm.

"I'm cold, Josh. Cold in my bones and in my heart. I won't never again feel the warm I felt in my sister Mary's kitchen with Will and the young'uns and the smell of good food and the laughin'. Never." A few tears trickled down her face. Too weary to brush them away herself, she felt Josh's rough hand gently wipe her cheek.

"I know, Nan," he said. "Ain't no turnin' back for none of us now."

As they cleared the stand of trees and crossed the open field toward the little cabin with one small candle flickering in the window, even Lady quickened her pace. The anticipation of warm shelter and food renewed their spirits.

"I'm so weary, I could sleep on top a picket fence," Nancy said to no one in particular as she urged Pepper forward.

"I reckon she'll find you somethin' better 'an that to sleep on. Might even have some vittles to quieten my growlin' belly." Luke spoke in a gruff voice, but Nancy knew he was pleased to see that all was well with Alice and the homestead.

Alice's and Luke's home was tiny—one sparse room with a loft above. It had none of the comforts that Nancy had grown used to at Will's and Mary's house and even at her own parents'. There was no stove to cook on, only a large open fireplace. A roughhewn table stood against one wall beneath the single window, and a low bed sagged in the corner. But the light from the one candle on the table and the warm fire made it a welcome homecoming. That early morning, after swallowing whatever warm food Alice placed in front of her, Nancy climbed the ladder to the loft and collapsed on a pile of straw and quilts in the corner, oblivious to the cold air which drifted through the chinks in the logs.

It was midday when Nancy finally emerged. Alice sat at her quilt frame, bending close to the cloth and stitching a fine line in the intricate patchwork. A shaft of sunlight shone across the material and over Alice's graying head. Nancy had the sudden urge to throw her arms around those bent shoulders. This was the one person now who was making a home for her. But Nancy also knew that Alice would gruffly shake off any show of affection. Instead she said, "That's a right pretty pattern, Alice."

"Thank you, child. It's one my granny showed me when I was a young'un. We can start one fer you this winter."

"I'd be much obliged, Alice," Nancy said softly.

Alice's kindly expression changed when she looked at Nancy. "Whenever you're about the house or farm, you mind you wear a skirt. If them Federals come nosin' 'round here and find you in britches, they'll know right off you're ridin' with the rangers. The two of us gotta look like harmless woman folk jist tendin' to the cookin' and farm work."

"Oh, I s'pose." Nancy groaned. As she turned to go up to the loft to change, she said, "When this here war's over, I'll never wear a skirt agin. All they do is tangle you up and slow ya' down."

"Lordy, girl," Alice laughed, "you know well as I do that you love traipsin' 'round in a pretty dress with your hair all clean and shinin' well as any young girl when there's fella's 'round to admire. Ain't you seen how Josh's eyes light up ever time you wear a dress?"

This time it was Nancy's turn to laugh. "Josh don't think of me as nothin' but a sister, Alice. And the captain sure don't seem to notice."

She was already at the top of the ladder to the loft, but Alice spoke loud enough for Nancy to hear. "Josh ain't lookin' at you like no brother, Nancy Hart."

When Nancy climbed back down, Alice had raised the quilting frame on the rope pulley close to the low ceiling beams. Josh stood by the table and was pulling jars of pickled eggs, preserved beans, some potatoes and onions, and a slab of smoked venison from a worn pack. "My ma sent some food supplies to keep you goin' for a few days," he said to Alice. "She knowed you wouldn't have nothin' put by since you been with the rangers all summer and autumn." He stopped talking when he saw Nancy and gave her a big grin. "How you feelin', Nan?"

She smiled back. "Rested a bit I reckon, Josh."

"Girl, you go on out and call Luke in," Alice said. "You and Josh'll want to hear his news from the captain."

"The captain?" Nancy asked. "Where's the captain?"

"Hush up, Nancy. You'll hear soon enough once you get Luke in here," Alice scolded.

Nancy hiked up her skirt and flew out the door to find Luke. A few minutes later she followed him into the cabin. He strode at his usual unhurried pace, while Nancy, face flushed and hands fluttering, tried to hurry him along. "Where did you see the captain? When did you see the captain?"

Ignoring her questions and proceeding to the fireplace, Luke took a chipped white china cup with a faded blue flowered pattern from the mantel. Intent, he lifted the coffee pot from its perch at the edge of the fire. Carefully he filled the china cup and carried it to the table, placing it in front of Alice. Nodding to Josh, he lifted three tin mugs from their hooks on the wall and filled them.

"Luke, tell me, what did the captain say?" Nancy was nearly dancing up and down with frustration.

Luke thrust a mug of coffee at Nancy. Josh pulled a stool out from the corner to a warm spot in front of the fire, and looking at Nancy, nodded towards it. "Blazes," Nancy muttered under her breath and sat on the stool. Josh leaned against the mantel and sipped his coffee.

Settling himself at the table next to Alice, Luke finally spoke. "The captain said...we're workin' outa our homes fer the time bein' instead of one central hideout, so we need a common signal. If the Home Guard or any of them Federalists is snoopin' 'round, we hang a quilt on the clothesline—as bold of colors as we can find to warn off any of the rangers that might be comin' our way. If there's a quilt flappin' in the breeze, make yourself scarce. It means them no good Home Guard is 'round."

"Where is the captain, Luke? And when did he tell you 'bout the quilt signal?" Nancy asked.

"I ain't finished yet. Jist listen," he replied. "The Moccasin Rangers are gonna strike and run, strike and run," Luke continued. "Calhoun County one mornin', Braxton that night, the next over to Webster, then down to Nicholas. The Federalists ain't gonna know how many we are or where we are. We're gonna keep 'em lookin' over their shoulder every minute. We'll scatter their horses, pull up railroad ties, burn trestles, pick off ever' sentinel, picket, or courier we come across. We'll make the country so unsafe for 'em, they won't never dare travel alone. They'll be so tied up here chasin' after us, they won't be botherin' Gen'ral Lee and our boys. Oh, I near forgot...Jeff Davis is duly elected president of the Confederacy, and we even got us a vice president name of Stephens."

Nancy's eyes widened as she listened.

"And we're operatin' outa our own places?" Josh asked.

"That's right," Luke answered. "So's after a raid, we scatter. They won't know where to look."

"Yeah, but what if the Federals do find me at my ma and pa's. They ain't part of the rangers, but the Home Guard won't care none 'bout that."

Alice touched Luke's arm. Their eyes met. Luke nodded to Alice and spoke. "We're beholdin' to yer folks fer sendin' us a supply of food to see us through this winter. But I spect it's best if you stay here with us. Don't wanna be endangerin' them." Luke paused, then went on, "And Nan, I know yer fond of Pepper, girl. But we couldn't have no horse with U.S. Cavalry on its rump holed up in our barn. Even a nearsighted nimcompoop of a Federal could see that. I had to pass him to our rangers who'll take him to Wise's boys behind the Confederate lines.

At least twenty-five or thirty rangers rode together that night, instead of the usual ten to fifteen. And among them were some faces, which Nancy did not recognize. Josh told her they were from George Downs' rangers, but they all seemed to know her. When Captain Conley instructed her to take charge of stampeding the horses in the Federal camp, the men did not object. Nancy noticed a new sense of respect and acceptance which she had never really felt before.

They were close now, and in unspoken accord, they slowed and stepped more carefully. A dull, cold heaviness was in the air. It would be snowing before dawn. A few campfires glowed, but most of the lights were extinguished as they approached the Federal camp near Sutton in Braxton County. An occasional gruff laugh, whinnying of horses, and the playing of a mouth organ could be heard.

This was Nathaniel's territory, and he, riding in the lead, halted them amidst a cluster of trees on a rise above the river and the camp. In a low whisper he spoke, "George, you and Patrick and Jackson head 'round to the left like we discussed. The guns and powder are in that long low buildin'. More 'an likely there'll be guards. Captain, the horses are corralled jist down yonder. Should be two pickets along the fence." And with that, Nathaniel and a third group split off to the right.

Nancy, Josh, and two others were left with Captain Conley. They could see in the dim light two figures leaning against the corral fence. The dark mass of horses occasionally shuffled and snorted, shifting slightly. The red glowing tip of a cigar arced through the darkness from hand to mouth and flared briefly as one of the men smoked.

The other yawned and said, "Ain't no stars tonight. Feels like snow. Most likely we'll have a coatin' afore morning."

"Ayuh," agreed the other picket. He shifted his body against the fence and took the cigar from his mouth. "Sure could stand a cup of hot coffee right about now."

A branch snapped under the hoof of one of the rangers' horses, and Nancy's heart stood still.

"Did you hear that?" the first picket spoke again. He straightened and reached for his gun which was propped against the fence.

"Warn't nothin'," said the smoker.

Nancy could see the dark bulk of the captain moving silently around the far side of the corral towards the men. Josh crept around on the other side, lower to the ground. A loud snort from one of the horses was answered with shuffling and interest from the corralled herd. And Nancy leaned down close to Lady to stroke her muzzle and quiet her.

Both pickets were standing upright now. The cigar was tossed to the ground and stomped out as they both looked around cautiously. "Don't like the sound of that," one said. "Feels like we're bein' watched."

"Halt! Who comes there?" the other called out. "Speak and identify yourself!"

"Don't mind if I do, gentlemen," said the captain as he suddenly loomed up behind the men, taking them both by surprise. And as if they were small boys, Captain Conley gripped them by the backs of their collars and with a swift hard upward swing, knocked their heads together. He let go, and their bodies crumpled to the ground like paper.

Bang! Pop! Pop! Bang! All at once the sounds of exploding ammunition filled the night. As flames leapt skyward off to her left casting an eerie light on the surroundings, Nancy spurred Lady forward. Josh and the captain pulled away the rails from the makeshift corral.

Nancy rode into the center of the milling horses. "Yah! Yah!" she shouted as she slapped horses on their rumps. Nancy maneuvered Lady around until they had all the horses moving in the same direction through the opened corral toward the middle of the camp. As other fires flared up and guns were shot, the frightened animals became more frantic. They spread out and moved faster and faster, trampling tents and anyone foolish enough to get in their way. All of Lady's instincts told her to run with the herd, but Nancy pulled on the reins and pressed her knee into the horse's side, skillfully turning her away from the stampeding herd and back toward the shelter of the woods along the river, the way they had come.

The pounding of the horses' hooves diminished as they ran farther and farther out of the camp and into the streets of the nearby town. It was all over in a few minutes. After the rangers had ridden a short distance out of the range of gunfire, they stopped and looked back. Fires still burned in the camp, flaring up here and there. They could see men silhouetted against the flames, scurrying with buckets of water. The captain's deep booming laugh rang out. Soon from Nancy's right other rangers joined in; then from her left more laughter, until the air was filled with the jeering, taunting sound which spilled down from the ridge and mingled with the soft snowflakes that had just begun to fall.

Chapter Ten

"Nancy, Captain has a job fer you," Luke said. "He wants you to meet him in Jenkin's wood near West Fork."

Still excited by the action of last night's raid, Nancy was full of questions. "Me? The captain wants me to do what, Luke?"

"Don't know, 'cept you're to have a bonnet and a basket of potatoes or apples or somesuch, like you was sellin'. He wants you there midday."

"But, but," she started, "I don't know where..."

Before she could continue, Luke interrupted. "Don't worry. Jist get yerself ready. I'll take you to Jenkin's wood."

Alice lifted a basket from a peg on the wall and began to fill it with onions and potatoes. She nodded toward the loft. "You go on, child, and git fixed up a bit. I'll ready the basket."

Nancy, filled with excitement, flew up to the loft. She could hear Alice and Luke whispering down below, but could not distinguish their words. Finally Luke raised his voice as he walked out the door. "Don't fret like a mother hen. She'll be fine. The captain'll see to that."

Alice's response was a loud "hrrumph."

Josh led Lady from the barn already saddled. Lady was restless, stepping sideways, head bobbing up and down, as if she, too, sensed more excitement in the air. She nuzzled at Nancy's head, knocking the bonnet back from her face.

Nancy laughed. "Lady, don't get so friendly jist when I'm aimin' to look like a proper farm girl."

Josh did not join in the laughter. He straightened her bonnet and briefly pressed his hand against her cheek. "You take care, Nan," he said softly.

Nancy's smile disappeared as she looked up at his somber expression. "I will, Josh."

Silently he helped her mount, handed up the basket of potatoes and onions, and slapped the horse on the rump. As she and Luke trotted away, Nancy turned and saw Josh standing by the rail fence, hands deep in his pockets, his hat pushed back on his head. She raised her hand in a farewell gesture. Josh merely nodded in response.

Several inches of snow had fallen in the night, but now the sun was out, melting the snowfall quickly. Luke, silent as usual, led Nancy to the edge of Jenkin's wood which bordered the West Fork of Stinson Creek. "I best make myself scarce," he said. "Don't want to be travellin' in groups the day after a raid. The captain knows you're here. Mind you, the road's jist to the side of the woods. Can you find your way back to the cabin?"

Nancy nodded in answer and looked eagerly around her for signs of the captain. Luke was quickly gone from sight, and Nancy sat alone on Lady. The only sounds were the rushing of the creek and the soft plops of melting snow as they fell from the branches to the ground. It couldn't have been more than a few minutes, but to Nancy those minutes stretched out. She adjusted the basket over the horn of her saddle, retied the strings of her bonnet a little tighter, and leaned down to croon in Lady's ear.

When she straightened up again, the captain was there only a few feet away and looking as much a giant as ever astride his horse. He grinned, knowing he had startled her and said, "You're a right pretty picture in that bonnet, Miss Nancy. Jist the way we want you to be for our Federalist friends." Then he was all business. Nancy's heart soared from the compliment as she tried to listen to what the captain was saying. "The Braxton Home Guard has been trackin' us since last night's raid. Took some of Downs' rangers and killed one of 'em."

Nancy involuntarily clutched at her throat. "Killed?"

"That's right. Now here's what I want you to do...The men might draw attention, but a young farm girl takin' vegetables to market in town won't be questioned. I want you to listen to any talk about town and pick up a newspaper if you can. I'll ride as far as the road with you, Nan, but then you're on your own." They had been moving as he talked, and now, just as they emerged from the thicket of woods into sight of the road, a mounted contingent of the Federal Home Guard came around the bend.

"Halt! Halt!" the lieutenant of the Home Guard shouted. "Fire!" The order was given, and within seconds a volley of shots blasted into the woods, splintering branches and sending twigs flying into the air. Lady reared up, and Nancy fought to control her, pulling on the reins and grasping the mane to keep herself from falling. Frantically she turned toward the captain, seeking some sort of help. All she saw was the flick of a chestnut tail as he and his horse disappeared into the woods. And then she was immediately surrounded by the soldiers. Rough hands pulled on Lady's bridle, and others jerked the reins from Nancy's hands.

Nancy's anger spilled out as she yanked her arm away from one of the men. "Keep your hands off me! How dare you shoot! You could've killed my horse!"

The soldier laughed out loud and reached again for her arm, but the officer in command barked out, "That's enough, Reeder. Leave the lady alone."

Nancy demanded again, "How dare you shoot at me!"

"Lieutenant Bender of the Braxton Home Guard, miss. You are our prisoner."

"Is this the treatment you give to a farm girl who's jist come avisitin' relatives?"

The lieutenant pulled his hat from his head and said, "I beg your pardon, miss, but you were in the company of that bushwhackin' Perry Conley, the well-known leader of the Moccasin Rangers, and we have orders to bring him and any of his companions in—whether they be breathin' and kickin' or not, miss. Beggin' your pardon."

Still feeling more anger than fear, Nancy flicked her hair from her face. Her bonnet had already fallen back on her shoulders. "Well, I don't know of no Connors, or who-ever you said. All's I know, he was gentlemanly enough to show me the way to the road when I got lost tryin' to take a shorter way inta Grantsville."

"Yes, well we'll talk further at headquarters, and we'll see what Captain Rollyson has to say about all that. You are our prisoner. Please state your name."

The fear was settling in now, and Nancy struggled to control the trembling in her voice. "Lieutenant, sir, I'm jist a farm girl, name of Ruth Ann Johnson, jist goin' about my business. And look what you done. All my vegetables are spilt and ruined." She looked down at the ground strewn with trampled potatoes and onions, the basket split in two.

They tethered Lady to the horse in front of Nancy and placed a mounted rider to her left and right and one behind. *No chance for escape. Even if I could get the reins, Lady couldn't outdistance all these men.* The soldier on her right was an older man, heavy set with tobacco juice trailing a thin line down the side of his mouth. He rode silently, occasionally spitting the drip-ping juice off to the side. *No help there.* On her left was a freckled-faced young man, tufts of bright red hair sticking out from under his cap. He was still beard-less, but soft patches of red-hued fuzz showed on his cheeks. Sensing a sympathetic ear, Nancy pulled her bonnet back up and tied it. Then, shaking her shoulders as if she were crying, she peeked out from under the brim of her bonnet to see the young man shift uncomfortably in his saddle. "Oh, my poor mama will be so worried," she murmured just loud enough for him to hear. She peeked again. She could see his Adam's apple bob up and down as he swallowed nervously. "Oh, poor Mama," Nancy sobbed louder this time.

"Don't fret, miss. Captain Rollyson will see you right." The young man spoke in an earnest voice.

Nancy turned her head toward him. "Do you really think so?" she asked with a shy smile.

The soldier on her right grunted, shook his head, and spit tobacco juice none too carefully on the ground between them.

As the troop entered the camp in Braxton County, Nancy was surprised by its size. *Blazes! It sure looks bigger in daylight. Jist look at all them blue bellies!* She grasped the saddle horn to stop her hands from shaking. Nancy felt that all eyes were on her. A man in buckskins and a wide-brimmed hat, cradling a rifle in his arm, walked across the path of the troops. *Is that the guide that nearly tracked me to the waterfall?* The tracker walked on without even glancing her way. *Calm, Nancy, calm. Keep yer head clear and think!*

Nancy was taken into a large house on the main street of the town. It had clearly once been the home of a prosperous family, but now was used as headquarters for the Federal Home Guard. Lieutenant Bender politely, but firmly led her up the front steps. "My horse! Where are you takin' my horse?" Nancy asked when she saw one of the men lead Lady away.

"Your horse will be properly cared for, miss," Lieutenant Bender said.

"But she's mine. I need her to get back home to my family!" Nancy was growing more frantic by the moment.

"If Captain Rollyson decides you are not aiding those bushwhackers of Conley's, your horse will be returned to you, Miss Johnson."

Nancy was at first taken by surprise when he called her by that name. He left her sitting on a hard bench in a small parlour off the main hall. The young, red-haired man stood guard at the doorway. *Johnson, Ruth Ann Johnson is my name,* she said repeatedly to herself. *I live on a farm near West Fork, and I was takin' my vegetables to market.*

Nancy suddenly realized she was very cold. She rubbed her hands together and stood up, cautiously looking at the guard. He stood straighter, lifting his rifle slightly. Nancy gave him a timid smile. "I'm jist cold, sir. I was fixin' to warm my hands by the fire." She motioned toward the few meager coals that burned in the open fireplace. "We been ridin' fer hours, sir, and I had only this shawl and bonnet fer warmth."

The young man looked embarrassed. He cleared his throat and swallowed, his Adam's apple bobbing up and down again. "I reckon I could build up the fire for you, miss. Wouldn't harm nothin'. I'm a bit cold myself," he said as he propped his rifle next to the door and knelt at the hearth.

"I'd be much obliged, sir." Nancy smiled again. "Could I call you by yer Christian name?"

"Emmett, miss. My name's Emmett."

"Emmett. That's a right nice name."

"Well...er...," he nodded, blushing so that the red of his face clashed with the copper of his hair. "They call me Rusty,...cause of this." And he blushed even redder as he touched his hair.

"Well, I would call you Emmett because it's such a right proper name fer you. It's plain to see yer mama learned you some manners." Nancy seated herself on the bench in front of the fire, crossing her knees and revealing a glimpse of petticoat and stocking above her laced shoes. She stretched out her hands to the growing warmth of the flames which now licked at the edge of the fresh wood he had thrown on the fire.

"You're supposed to be standin' guard! Not lollygaggin' 'round in here," the older soldier shouted as he entered the room and picked up Emmett's rifle.

Emmett jumped from his crouched position. "I was j-j-j-just stirrin' up the f-f-f-fire, Corporal," he stuttered.

"Leavin' your post and weapon is a court-martial offense, you weak-kneed nimcompoop." He thrust the rifle roughly into Emmett's hands.

"He was jist makin' the room a bit warmer fer me," Nancy started. "You see, I only have this shawl an..."

As though she had not spoken, the older soldier turned his back, ignoring her completely. Nancy listened as he continued to curse Emmett's stupidity. "Don't go forgettin' your duty at the first flash of a pretty petticoat. She's a prisoner and a secesh at that. You know you can't trust a one of them."

Emmett spoke in a low voice. "Aw, she ain't no secesh, Miller. She's jist a farm girl who had some bad luck and got lost."

"Humph, bad luck. Bad luck to be anywheres near that snake, Conley. It ain't for you to decide. It's up to Captain Rollyson. Listen here what it says in the *Gazette* 'bout that bushwhacker and his cutthroats." The corporal began to read haltingly from a newspaper, stumbling over some words. "After setting fire to the ammunition store, resulting in mmm...multiple explosions, knocking two guards un...ccconscious, stampeding fifty horses and causing great danger to life and limb of our brave Home Guard ['that's us'], the scurr...scurr..."

Emmett looked at the word where the corporal had placed his finger on the printed page. "Scurr-i-lous," he pronounced slowly, "that's the word."

Miller continued, "...scurrilous attackers fled for cover into the nearby hills where they paused long enough to fill the night air with ghostly, der-i-sive laughter. Mingled with the male voices, the clear soprano of female laughter could be heard." Miller tilted his head in Nancy's direction as he drew out the word female.

Nancy, who had been openly listening to the entire conversation, turned her head back to the heat of the fire to hide the instant flush of her face. *Female laughter. Be calm. Be calm. There's plenty of females 'round these parts. I ain't the only one. I'm jist a farm girl, name of Ruth Ann.*

A nearby door opened and closed. Footsteps approached. The corporal and Emmett forgot the newspaper article and stood at attention. "Come this way, Miss Johnson," Lieutenant Bender said. "Captain Rollyson will see you now."

On shaky legs, Nancy followed him across the hall. Captain Rollyson sat at a desk facing the door, but he did not look up directly. He appeared to be reading some papers.

"Captain Rollyson, sir," Lieutenant Bender began. "This is Miss—"

Abruptly the captain cut him off. "Lieutenant, allow the lady to introduce herself."

"Yes, sir," Lieutenant Bender stepped aside, at the same time gently prodding Nancy forward by the arm until she stood directly in front of the desk. Her heart was pounding so forcefully she was sure he could see her chest moving. Her mouth felt like cotton.

"So," the captain said as he rose from behind the desk. He was a tall man with a long face. Pince-nez eyeglasses perched on the end of his ample nose. He peered at Nancy over the top of them. "Have a seat. Have a seat," he said, walking from around the desk, hands behind his back. He stopped near the chair where Nancy had uneasily placed herself. "State your name."

"Sir, I was only tryin' to sell my vegetables," she began.

"Your name, please." Captain Rollyson was standing behind her chair now, so she could not see him.

"It's Ruth Ann Johnson, sir." Nancy barely whispered the words.

"What's that? I cannot hear you."

"Ruth Ann Johnson," she said louder and more firmly.

"Hmmm, Johnson. Of the Harry Johnson family or one of Walter's clan?"

Nancy's eyes widened. Frantically she tried to recall the names Josh had mentioned the day they drove the wagon. *Was there a Harry or a Walter? Is the captain tryin' to trick me?* "Well, sir," Nancy said uncertainly, "I reckon I'm related somehow to most of the Johnsons in Calhoun County. I have a brother, name of Billy. But the truth is, my pa had a fallin' out with the family, and he don't talk none 'bout the rest of the family or 'low us to see 'em."

"And where do you live, Miss Johnson?"

"In Calhoun County, over to the valley beyond Stinson Creek."

"How old are you?"

"I'm fifteen, sir." The questions were coming so quickly now, she barely had time to answer.

"Miss Johnson, what were you doing in the company of Perry Conley?" Captain Rollyson made a full circle around Nancy's chair and seated himself once more at his desk. He moved the spectacles up higher on his nose and stared at Nancy's face as she answered.

Blazes, those eyes can see right through me and out the other side. "I already told the lieutenant."

"Well, please tell me." Rollyson leaned back in his chair, but never took his eyes from Nancy's.

"I don't know nothin' 'bout no Connors."

"Conley," Captain Rollyson corrected.

"All I know is I got lost in the woods tryin' to save time goin' to Grantsville, and a nice fella' showed me the way to the road, and my poor mama's gonna be so worried if I don't git home afore dark."

"You had never seen him before?"

"No, sir." Nancy shook her head.

"Where were you last night?"

"At home with my mama, sir. She's been feelin' poorly."

"And where did you learn to handle a horse so expertly?"

"From my pa. I been ridin' almost afore I could walk."

"My lieutenant said you brought your horse under control immediately in the midst of gunfire."

"I been huntin' with my brother all my growin' up years, sir." Nancy's voice was quivering now. It was so hard to keep her fear under control with the relentless questioning.

"Are you acquainted with the Moccasin Rangers, Miss Johnson?"

"No, sir," Nancy shook her head again. A tear slid down her cheek.

"Oh come now, Miss Johnson. Surely there's not a soul in western Virginia that is not acquainted with the notorious Moccasin Rangers."

"I heard tell of them, sir. I only meant I don't know none of them." Her chin began to tremble, and even though she fought for control, Nancy could no longer hold back her tears. She turned her head to the side, wiping at her eyes with the corner of her shawl.

Captain Rollyson stared at her a moment longer; then he stood. "Lieutenant."

"Sir." Lieutenant Bender came to attention.

"See that Miss Johnson has her mount returned and is escorted as far as the Calhoun County line."

"Yes, sir."

"Sorry to have detained you, miss," Captain Rollyson said as he removed his spectacles. "But these Rebel bushwhackers are evil men and very dangerous. Best you stay clear of them. If you make haste, you will be home to your mama before dark."

Nancy nodded and muttered a small "thank you."

Without comment, Lieutenant Bender held out a clean white handkerchief to Nancy; then he guided her from the room.

Chapter Eleven

Nancy was riding Lady back toward Calhoun County. She wanted to spur her on as fast as she could back to freedom and the warm safety of Alice and Luke and Josh. This time she was not held as a prisoner on a lead, escorted on all sides. But she was escorted by the shy Emmett at a slow and proper pace for a young farm girl in skirt and petticoats. The sun in the late November sky was sinking low, and Nancy knew she had less than an hour of daylight. It was all she could do to rein Lady in and try to carry on polite conversation with Emmett.

"I'll be happy to see you all the way home, Miss Ruth Ann," Emmett spoke earnestly to Nancy as they rode along.

"Thank you kindly, Emmett, but Lady knows the road from here. She'll get me home safe and sound."

"You and your ma will soon be safe for certain. I heard tell there's a Captain Simpson outa Parkersburg that's puttin' together a company to flush all the bushwhackers outa these hills."

Nancy caught her breath. She spoke slowly, carefully controlling each word. "How do you know 'bout that, Emmett?"

Seeing that he had caught Nancy's interest, Emmett cleared his throat and spoke in a deeper, more self-important voice. "Why, I heard it from the sergeant, who heard it from the lieutenant. Yes sir, a whole company. They'll climb all over these hills and shake out all them raiders and marauders. No need to worry, Miss Ruth Ann. The Federal army is here to help and protect you." With this last statement, he sat straighter in the saddle and thrust out his chest.

"That is reassurin', Emmett. And will you ride with 'em?" she asked innocently.

"Oh no. These troops'll be outa Camp Pierpont up Elizabeth way."

"We sure will feel protected with 'bout a hundred boys in blue ridin' our hills."

Emmett laughed. "Well, won't be nothin' like a hundred for a while yet. Maybe thirty or so to start. But they'll do the job just the same."

"When can me and Mama 'spect to feel all safe agin?" Nancy asked softly.

"I reckon by Christmas it should be peaceable 'round here." Then swallowing hard and lowering his head, Emmett asked, "Would you and your mama welcome a visitor 'bout that time?"

Avoiding an answer to the question, Nancy scanned the road ahead. There was a lone figure approaching on horseback. *Josh?* "Emmett, I think that's my brother Billy come lookin' fer me." Louder, she shouted toward the rider whom she was now sure was Josh. "Billy! Is that you, Billy?" She waved her hand. Josh was close enough now that she could see a strand of his whitish hair beneath his hat, hanging lank across his eyes. She spurred Lady forward, placing as much distance between herself and Emmett as possible. She reached Josh while Emmett was still behind her and quickly whispered, "I'm Ruth Ann." Then in a loud voice she said,. "Billy, I knowed you and Mama would be frettin' over me. I been carried all the way to Braxton County fer questionin' 'bout them Moccasin Rangers. But I done told that Captain Rollyson that us Johnsons don't hold with them rangers."

Emmett moved beside her. "This here's my brother, Billy Johnson. Billy, this is Emmett who was seein' me home." Emmett nodded and extended his hand.

Avoiding a handshake, Josh touched the brim of his hat and murmured, "Much obliged."

"Thank you kindly, Emmett. Me and my fam'ly will look forward to that peaceable Christmas, jist like you said." And without delaying any further, Nancy and Josh left the bewildered, red-faced young soldier behind.

"Nan," Josh began in a whisper.

"Shhh," Nancy cautioned as she looked back over her shoulder to wave to Emmett. The gesture seemed to rouse the smitten soldier. He turned his horse and slowly trotted down the road.

Nancy and Josh did not speak until they were deep into the woods. And the farther Nancy got from Emmett and Braxton County and the Federals, the more the fear and anxiety, which she had held in check for so long, threatened to overwhelm her. Finally, shaking almost uncontrollably, Nancy stopped Lady and slumped forward.

Josh drew up next to her, leaning in closely and wrapping an arm around her. "It's all right, Nan. It's all right. You did fine. It's over."

The tears were started now, and at first she could not speak over the sobs. Finally she managed to say, "It was so hard, Josh. I was so skairt. And the captain! Josh, Captain Conley jist left me! He hightailed right outa there, leavin' me behind. And they asked me so many questions. And I had to think. I had to keep thinkin' all the time, so's I wouldn't make no mistakes. And I thought they would take Lady and I'd never get back to you and Alice and Luke."

"Shhh, Nan. It's all right."

"And the captain jist left me; left me all alone. I never would've thought..."

"I'd have stayed with you, Nan. I'll never leave you." Pushing the bonnet back from her head, Josh ran his hand over her hair. "I'll never leave you, Nan," he repeated.

In the dim light of dusk, long purple shadows, cast by the trees, fell across the frozen ground. The breath of the horses formed into steamy vapor in the frigid evening air. A few flakes of snow floated around them. Side by side the two riders moved through the woods, stopping at the edge of the clearing. The snow fell harder now, swirling on the breath of the wind. In the distance they could see the cabin. A light flickered brightly in the window. Smoke rose from the chimney, spreading the scent of burning pinewood. Lady shook her head and whinnied, pawing the ground impatiently, anxious for the warmth of the barn and her feedbag. Somewhere behind them an owl hooted. Josh reached over and held Nancy's hand. "We're home."

When Nancy opened the door to the cabin, Alice was bent over the quilt frame, stitching a line in the dim candle light. "Nancy, child, yer safe!" She rose, dropping her needle and knocking over the frame. She reached out her hands, and Nancy went into her quick, firm embrace, tears threatening again. But Alice was immediately back to her usual stoic self and turned to stir up the fire. "Best get yerself warmed up whilst I get some vittles fer you. I been frettin' over you this long day."

Luke was sitting by the fire. He took his pipe from his mouth, and a fleeting smile crossed his lined face. Alice continued, "Josh went out a lookin' fer you. Once we got word from the captain 'bout what happened, there was no holdin' him down. He was rantin' and ravin' 'bout the captain leavin' you on yer own even though Luke told him that you was best off without Conley."

"Josh is seein' to the horses," Nancy interrupted.

Luke, standing now, poured steaming coffee into a mug and handed it to Nancy. "Here, this'll warm yer hands and yer insides." He seated her in his own chair beside the fire.

Nancy took a sip of the hot coffee, and then leaned her head back, closed her eyes, and sighed. "I'm so tuckered, but I got news."

"What news?" Luke asked.

"Let the girl catch her breath and git some vittles inside her," Alice protested.

Ignoring his wife, Luke repeated, "What news?" A burst of cold air swept through the doorway as Josh entered, stamping his feet and brushing snow from his shoulders. "What is your news, girl?" Luke asked impatiently as he handed another mug of coffee to Josh. When Alice started to speak in protest, Luke raised his hand, palm outward, to silence her.

"There's a Captain Simpson outa Parkersburg bringin' a company of Federals jist special to git all us Moccasin Rangers outa these hills. He's got about thirty men already, more a comin', and 'spects to have it all done by Christmas."

Luke was pulling on his boots and reaching for his coat. He nodded to Josh, "The captain needs to know this." And the two men headed out into the snowy night.

On the morning of November 28, Nancy woke earlier than usual to sounds of movement and conversation down below. She dressed hastily, combed her hair and quickly plaited it. Josh and Luke were dressed as if for a raid and were washing down the last of breakfast with cups of coffee when she came down the ladder.

"Where you headed?" Nancy asked. "Why didn't you wake me? I'll jist go put my britches on."

"No, girl," Luke said. "The captain said no women-folk this time."

"But I ain't—"

"Nan," Josh interrupted, "you need to stay with Alice this time. You may be needed here. It's that Captain Simpson you told us about. Yesterday, he left Camp Pierpont with nigh up to thirty men and made a clean sweep all along Little Kanawha River, arrestin' anyone they heard tell might be a ranger or be helpin' in any way. They picked up Patrick Rafferty and Jackson Wright and more of Downs' men without a shot fired. And now they're movin' this way."

Nancy was speechless. Her hands clutched at her throat.

Luke continued. "Captain Conley is gettin' everyone he can together from our group and any others to head them blue bellies off."

"Then he needs me, too," Nancy insisted.

"No, Nan," Josh said again. "The Federals are payin' visits to the homes, and you need to be here with Alice in fittin' clothes fer a woman. Don't go tryin' no heroics on your own."

"We best be getting' on, boy," Luke said to Josh. "The sun'll be up afore long."

Josh gave Nancy's arm a quick squeeze and before she knew it, both men were gone. Nancy threw herself down in Luke's rocker in front of the fire.

"Don't mean to disturb you none, ma'am, but me and some of my men are patrollin' hereabouts, and we'll be needing our midday meal." The soldier filled the doorway, his bulky frame shutting out the scant winter light.

Alice with a firm and steady voice responded, "Come in or out. Yer chillin' the place. How many are you?"

"Just me and three others, ma'am." His eyes rested on Nancy, and he smiled, showing a yellow gap-toothed grin. "Me and my men would be obliged for your hospitality. Your men folk not about the place?" he asked, his narrow eyes darting about the small room.

"You and yer men get over yonder to the barn outa the cold, and I'll see to feedin' you."

"Oh, I think it's much warmer in here," he said and stepped toward the table where Nancy was standing. She was frozen to the spot, her eyes wide. The sleeve of the blue uniform brushed against her as the soldier moved to the chair. He tipped his hat, but did not remove it. "Well tarnation, who'd have thought a pretty little lady like you lived here?" he said, cracking his horse-toothed smile at Nancy.

Alice placed herself between Nancy and the man. "We'll be glad to help out our fightin' men, but we got our own chores to keep up, too." Then squeezing Nancy by the upper arm to bring her back to her senses, Alice continued. "Girl, you go up above and take that old quilt out fer a good airin', and tell them others out there to come on in and git some vittles."

Nancy, alert now, moved quickly to the ladder and pulled the quilt down from the loft. Wrapping a shawl about her shoulders, she went outside. "My ma said to come in and git yer meal," she told the three who stood beside their horses, stamping their feet and blowing on their hands. *Blazin' blue bellies,* she thought. *At least these ain't like ol' horseface inside, sittin' at Luke's place. Luke and Josh! Oh, what if they come back afore we get rid of this passel of varmints!* Quickly she placed the quilt across the line and secured it with wooden pegs. The brisk wind caught it and snapped the quilt up and down, a bright colored warning flag. Nancy stood shivering with her arms wrapped around her, looking off in the direction Josh and Luke had ridden before dawn—the same direction these Federals had come just now. Her face stung from the cold wind, and she turned to go back to help Alice. "Blasted blue bellies," she said aloud in disgust before she opened the door.

The Federals filled the room with their big, blue-uniformed bodies. One of the men stood up when she entered, knocking his chair back against the wall. The other men laughed loudly. Nancy refused to look anyone of them in the eye. Holding her skirt close to her body so that not a stitch would brush across the boot of ol' horseface, she stepped carefully over the outstretched leg. Alice dipped out a bowl of the stew which was kept simmering over the fire and placed it before the sergeant. *So much for our own supper,* Nancy thought, *and that plump squirrel Josh brought home yesterday afternoon.* Nancy placed three more bowls before the other men. Horseface spooned a large helping of food into his mouth. Immediately his eyes grew big and his face red. He spat the whole mouthful back into the bowl.

"Too hot for you, Sarge?" one of the men asked, laughing.

He nodded, unable to speak, his eyes watering.

"What you need is a mouthful of that snow outside to cool your tongue off," another said as he blew on his own spoonful before tasting it.

Horseface stood, grabbing Alice's blue and white teacup from the mantelpiece and opened the door, letting in a gust of frigid air as he leaned down to scoop up a cup of the fresh snow. Tilting his head back, he gulped the snow into his burning mouth.

"Hey, Sarge, close the door. You're coolin' off ours, too," one of the younger men called. The others laughed. Horseface grunted in response and leaned down to refill the cup. When the door was closed and the sergeant sat once again to eat, Alice placed a tin mug of spring water in front of him. She reached for the china cup, but before her fingers touched it, the sergeant's large hand came down and engulfed it, as if to say, "Leave it there." Alice turned back to the fire, and Nancy went to stand next to her as all four men devoured their meal.

"This is right tasty, ma'am," one of the younger men commented. Alice merely nodded.

They were scraping the last from the bowls when a distant burst of gunfire was heard. The men looked up in surprise and, after a brief silent moment, scrambled to their feet, grabbing their guns and coats. In the flurry of the moment as they hurriedly left, the china cup was knocked to the floor. And horseface, gruffly saying, "Much obliged," unheedingly stepped on the scattered fragments, crushing them into the planks.

The room was empty, the door still hanging open, and the volleys of gunfire continued, as the Federals galloped off in the direction of the noise. But all Nancy saw were the crushed fragments of the fine, blue and white teacup on the rough wooden floor. She knelt, carefully picking up the larger pieces and trying to fit them together in some semblance of a cup. "Oh Alice, maybe Luke could...," Nancy began.

"Hush, girl," Alice said gruffly, "it's beyond fixin'." She walked briskly to the door, closed and bolted it. Then she took the broom from the corner. Nancy still knelt on the floor, holding the handle of the cup. Alice swept the remaining fragments into a tiny pile, and when Nancy looked up, she saw one tear trailing down Alice's lined cheek.

The sounds of battle went on and on, seemingly for hours, but by the old clock on the mantel not more than three-quarters of an hour. Alice and Nancy did not speak, but went about cleaning up the scattered mess left by the Federals and washing the dishes. Nancy's eyes kept returning to the window. "No sign of them yet, Alice. I wish I knew where the fightin' was and if they're in it."

"Ain't no use a wishin', girl. They know how to take care of theirselves."

Finally there was silence. And the silence loomed louder than the gunfire. Nancy wrapped her shawl around her head and shoulders and took the empty bucket to the springhouse to fill it. Outside the silence lay even heavier. She saw the quilt hanging limp now on the line, and she stopped to unpeg it and fold it to bring inside. Then a half-dozen rapid shots sounded. The gunfire was not returned. Nancy ran inside, and as the echo of the sound faded, the women turned toward each other. Their eyes met, and without speaking, they embraced. They stood clinging to each other, clinging to life, waiting for the sound of further gunfire. None came.

Luke and Josh did not return that long afternoon and night and the next long day. They heard no news. Nancy kept thinking of the endless hours she and Mary had waited for news of Will. The awful picture of his final return, draped on the back of the horse, loomed ever present in her mind. *It can't happen to Josh or Luke. It jist can't,* she told herself over and over.

"Frettin' won't git nothin' done, girl," Alice said. "Let's start piecin' that quilt fer you."

Now Nancy pulled the cover up to her nose. Her back still ached from the hours spent leaning over the table to cut quilt squares. She lay on the straw-filled mattress and looked through the tiny square of the loft window as clouds passed in front of the full moon, then disappeared from view. The wind howled outside and she heard Alice poke at the fire down below. Although Alice had told her during the past days that Luke and Josh could take care of themselves, she noticed that Alice had not slept much and kept a candle burning in the window.

She dreamed she was with Josh in his special place on the mountain. She heard his laughter, and when she opened her eyes, the full moon was replaced by a gray, predawn sky outside the little window. Again she heard the laugh. "Josh! It's not a dream. It's Josh." Her bare feet were on the ladder. She pulled the quilt behind her as she half stumbled, half ran to the fireplace where he sat. As soon as he saw her he stood, arms open. Then he was holding her. All wrapped in the quilt and in Josh's arms, she had never felt so warm or so content. "Where have you been? What happened?" Nancy asked, pushing away from Josh and for the first time seeing Luke propped up atop the bed.

"'Bout time you noticed me," Luke grumbled. A large poke bonnet, still tied around his neck, was pushed back from his head, and his face was shaved clean. And strangest of all, he wore a huge calico dress, belted in at the waist and stuffed full about his chest.

Laughter bubbled up from deep inside Nancy and took hold of her until she couldn't stop. "You do look quite fetchin', ma'am," she said between bursts of laughter. It seemed to be contagious because now Josh and Alice, too, were nearly doubled with laughter.

"Aww, it ain't that peculiar," Luke said, but even he lay chuckling on the bed.

Finally, wiping tears from her eyes and sitting down in the rocker, Nancy hugged the quilt closer and tucked her feet under her. "Now, please tell me what happened, and why in tarnation are you dressed like an ol' lady, Luke?"

"Josh, you tell it," Luke said as he bit into one of Alice's biscuits and drank deeply from his mug of coffee. He reached to pat Alice's hand as she sat contentedly beside him on the bed.

"Well, the captain mustered all our men and some of both Wilson's and Downs' rangers. I reckon we had 'bout fifty men or so, don't you think, Luke?" Josh asked, and Luke nodded, his mouth full.

"And jist about noon we come upon Simpson's group at that blue belly sympathizer, Adonijah McDonald's home. 'Course the Federals don't see us; we're back in the woods and they're out there plain as day, swarmin' all over the roads. Well, Adonijah comes out, all hospitable, and invites Simpson and his men to dine with him. And since there's so many of them, Simpson accepts for him and some of his officers, but sends the others to neighborin' farms to beg their noon meal."

At that, Alice gave a loud "hrumph." Josh stopped and looked questioningly at her, but Alice just said, "Go on."

"Well, they all scatter out, and of course this looks like a situation made to order fer us. So Captain Conley has us move in, and he shouts out a demand for Simpson to surrender. Not that we thought he would, 'cause they start firin' on us, and we open up back at them.

Blazes, what a battle. I ain't never been in one like that afore. It went on and on."

"Waste of good gunpowder, if you ask me," said Luke. "Firin' over and over on a house."

"We heard it," Nancy murmured, "and hoped you wasn't in it."

"After awhile the captain signaled us to pull back. It was then that I knew Luke was shot through the leg."

"Shot!" Nancy exclaimed and started to rise from the rocker.

Luke held up his hand. "I'm here now, ain't I, girl? Go on, Josh."

"Luke leaned on his rifle, I helped him, and we hobbled through the woods to our horses. When we was far enough inta the woods we stopped, and I cut away Luke's trouser and bound up the leg to try to stop the bleedin'. He was gettin' kinda' weak and I knew we had to git some help."

"Where was the others?" Nancy asked as she pulled the quilt tighter around herself.

"They was all scattered. Well, we come by the Morton place. Granny Morton knows me and my kin. She's got a son off fightin' with Jackson's men. Anyhow, she settled us in her barn, tended to Luke's leg, and put a good yarrow poultice on it."

"It's closing up real fine now," Luke added.

Josh continued, "The Federals came 'round to her house, lookin' fer them 'Rebel bushwhackers.' And she, calm as molasses, told 'em she ain't seen no bushwhackers, but she sure would be on the lookout and let 'em know if'n she does. We were bidin' our time there, 'cause we knew the Federals would be watchin' fer a while after the battle, but we didn't want to put Granny in danger. The only way to git home was out in the open. We reckoned maybe one farmer could git through, but two men together would draw attention. Luke couldn't travel alone, 'cause of his wound. So I colored my hair with tea, pulled my hat down on my head and was ready. Luke was more of a problem. Granny dressed him in one of her dresses, tied a poke bonnet on his head, and put her ol' spectacles on his nose. Luke sat side saddle on her ol' mule, all covered by the dress and bonnet and hunched over. Pretty soon we come to a patrol guardin' the road outa town. 'Halt,' he says, so we stopped. 'What is your business?' 'I'm in a powerful hurry, sir,' I says. 'It's my wife's birthin' time, and I'm bringin' Granny Morton to help her out.' I look over and see Luke slumpin' low in the saddle, and my heart starts beatin' faster."

Nancy could see that Josh was caught up in the tellin' of the story. She had never heard him say so much at one time.

"'Well,' says the blue belly real slowlike, 'I got to get yer name and destination afore I ken let you pass.' While he was gettin' his paper ready and lickin' his graphite, I spoke up. 'Granny, my Susan is powerful poorly. You ride on ahead to her and I'll answer these here questions.' Without waitin' fer the soldier to answer, I slapped the rump of Granny's ol' mule, and he plodded on. I could see Luke's hand, white with hangin' onto the saddle fer dear life. They didn't stop him, and soon he disappeared 'round the bend in the road ahead."

"Well, it's all over now, and yer back safe." Alice smiled at Luke as she spoke.

"That ain't exactly true. You ain't heard the worst yet." Josh put his head down. The room was very quiet. "Nathaniel was shot," he continued in a low voice. "When me an' Luke was hobblin' inta the woods, I seen Nathaniel drag hisself over to a chestnut tree and prop hisself up. I thought the captain and the others seen it and would go fetch him." Josh's voice dropped lower to nearly a whisper. "I was helpin' Luke onta his horse when we heard the shots. 'Bout six of 'em all at once. Those cursed Federals didn't take prisoners like any fighin' man with honor would do. They jist shot down a wounded man." Josh put his head down. Nancy reached out to touch his shoulder.

"If I could've walked myself," Luke began.

"Hush, Luke, it weren't yer fault, nor Josh's neither," Alice said. "It's jist how it is when yer fightin' varmints that don't go by no rules but their own."

The room became silent once more. The fire dimmed to low glowing embers. For a long time no one moved to build it up again.

Chapter Twelve

For the next few weeks well into December, they stayed close about the cabin and small farm. Josh ventured out only to the surrounding woods to do some hunting, and Alice kept Luke as confined as she could while his wound continued to heal. One afternoon a small contingent of Federal troops rode through the valley at a distance. Nancy heard them before she saw the mass of blue coats. Her heart beat faster, and her mouth grew dry. *What if it's that horse-toothed sergeant again?* But they did not veer off their path.

Nancy had begun to piece the quilt squares that she and Alice had cut. She found that she did not mind the hours of intricate stitching as the wedding ring pattern took form. Sewing had been one of the few household chores she actually enjoyed. Not mending or darning, of course, but the actual planning and making of a quilt or dress. Just as Luke might start with a plank of wood and cut and build and smooth it to a finished piece of furniture, Nancy felt satisfaction in the placing of the small scraps of cloth one by one, blending the colors and forming the patterned coverlet that was not only beautiful, but useful.

Still, as the days passed, she longed to be riding Lady, flying free across Will's and Mary's meadow as she had so many months ago. She ached to know what had become of Mary and the young'uns—Ginny, Lou, John, and baby Margaret—and also of the new little baby, whose name she did not even know and who would never know the love of his father, Will. When these thoughts became too heavy and she could not keep the tears from stinging her eyes, she would have to leave the sewing and go outside to draw icy water from the spring or to carry armloads of firewood until the cold and physical exertion would drive all the thoughts from her mind.

In the last week of December, Luke came in from hunting, dangling two pheasants from a rope. "Got fresh fowl fer Christmas dinner here," he announced as he held them out. Alice gladly received the offering and immediately began preparations for the next day's meal. "Got somethin' else," he said, looking at Nancy who was busy stitching the quilt. He shook snow from his coat, hung it up, and pulled a crumpled envelope from his pocket. "Came by way of hand to hand. Finally Granny Morton got hold of it and passed it among some of the rangers. Them that's got book learnin' say it's fer a Mistress Nancy Hart. Do we know a body by that name?" Luke asked, holding the envelope high in the air.

Alice stopped her work and turned to stare at the envelope. Nancy sat motionless. For a moment she could not speak. Then excitement overwhelmed her. "A letter for ME?" she shreaked, reaching for the small envelope. It was wrinkled and smudged with dirt. She took it and turned it over in her hands slowly, almost as if she could feel the words she knew were inside. She did not know what the words meant, but she recognized the script. The large round loops waving across the face of the envelope were in her sister's handwriting. "Mary! It's a letter from Mary!" She ran to the peg and pulled her shawl down, wrapping it around her shoulders.

"Where you goin' girl? It's snowin' and sleetin' out there." But Nancy did not heed Luke's or even Alice's call of "Nancy, he's not there. He's a huntin'."

"Josh!" she called as she ran toward the barn. The sleet and snow swirled around her and stung her face. "Josh!" she called again, but no answer came.

Lady, hearing her voice and thinking she was about to be fed, pawed the ground and snorted a greeting from her stall. "Oh, where is he, Lady? Where did he get to jist when I need him most?" She pulled the letter from under her shawl and looked at it again. Her heart beat faster. *How long ago did Mary send the letter? Mary and the young'uns, are they all right?* Nancy held the envelope against her heart and closed her eyes. In her mind she could hear Mary's voice, "They won't let you stay, little sister. When they see a young girl, they'll jist send you packin'." Nancy smiled as she remembered. Now she placed the letter under her shawl, gave the disappointed Lady a gentle pat, and walked back to the cabin. Later, as dinner was simmering over the fire, Nancy exploded. "Oh, where in bloomin' blazes is he?" she shouted.

Luke, who had been dozing in his chair, snapped his head up. "Huh? What?" he asked.

"Nancy, yer gonna wear a path to that window a lookin' out. Sides, it's a might dark now to see. He'll come home when he comes home," Alice said, annoyed at the outburst.

"I ain't never again gonna need to wait on another body to know what's mine to know," Nancy vowed as she looked again at the writing on the envelope. She sat on the bench and folded her arms across her chest to wait for Josh.

Her neck was stiff from the cold and from dozing on and off while sitting on the hard chair. The room was quiet except for the sounds of Luke's snoring and Alice's steady breathing. *Blast and blazes, where is he?* Nancy moved to the fireplace and poked at the embers. She placed another log on the fire and rubbed her hands, waiting for the warmth to flow from the new flames. She returned to the table and extinguished the small candle which burned there. The light from the fire now brightened the room. Nancy thought, *It ain't jist that I need him to read me my letter. What if he's hurt out there? What if he ain't comin' back?* She stared through the single window at the blackness of the night. Her eyes were tired and she struggled to keep them open. Finally, a light pierced the darkness. It bobbed through the black night toward the house, and she knew it had to be Josh carrying the lantern from the barn. Nancy rushed to the door and flung it open, letting in a gust of cold air which sent the flames in the fireplace jumping high.

"I thought you'd be asleep." Josh smiled as he entered the room.

"Where you been, Josh? I was skairt you wasn't comin' home!"

"Nan, I told you I'd never leave you, " Josh said, and he pulled her close. Nancy felt the chill of his coat and the wetness from the snow, but she did not care. She simply closed her eyes and leaned on him. After awhile, he spoke into her hair. "I been to see my folks. Givin' it's Christmas, my ma wouldn't forgive me if she didn't see me. Oh, I nearly forgot." He pushed Nancy gently away from him and reached into the pocket of his coat. "I brought you this." He placed an orange in her hand. "Happy Christmas, Nan."

Nancy held it carefully in both hands as if Josh had handed her a treasure. "An orange," she said. "I ain't never tasted one afore, but I smelt 'em," and she put it up to her nose, breathing in deeply. "In Liam Kelley's gen'ral store, he had 'em in a barrel always 'round Christmas time, and Miz Kelley always had some of the peelin's in a bowl on the counter. But Ma said, 'Twas a luxury we couldn't afford.'"

"Well, now you can, Nan," Josh said. He hung his coat on the peg and, taking the orange, used the knife from his pocket to cut into the fruit. Juice ran down his hand, and he laughed as he licked the side of his fingers. "Here." He offered her a quarter of the orange. "Just eat the inside part."

"I got me a letter today, from my sister, I think. Will you read it to me?"

Josh placed the fruit on the table between them. He rubbed his hands clean on his trousers and took the precious envelope from Nancy. Leaning closer to the light from the lantern, he said, "It's from Mary Price to you." Then he carefully opened the envelope and unfolded the single page. "My dear sister Nancy," he began.

Nancy nodded her head and moved forward on the bench anxious to hear every word. "I ain't much at letter writin', but there's things that need to be said. I know you must be frettin' 'bout what's become of me and the young'uns jist as I been frettin' 'bout you. First, I want you to know I hold no grudge nor blame against you for what happened, though I reckon others here abouts do, and it's best you stay away. Ma and Pa done gone back to Tazewell, and the young'uns and me are fixin' to move on to Kentucky to live with our brother, John. Harley Hughes, next farm over, has offered a fair price for all. As it is now late November, I hope to have us settled afore hard winter sets in. I heard tell Colonel Poole was shot dead right in front of his tent, and it made me wonder, though be sure I didn't say nothin'. The baby is named William and has his papa's eyes. I am sore grieved without my Will and without my sister. God bless you. In hopes this letter will find you afore the year is out, your loving sister, Mary Price."

Josh laid the letter down and looked at Nancy staring into the fire. The wind howled around the chimney. "I ain't never gonna see her agin, Josh, or the young'uns," Nancy finally said softly. She wiped tears from her cheek as she spoke. "I can't even write her no letter. I been foolish, Josh. I never had time for book learnin', too busy ridin' or huntin' with Pa and my brothers to pay attention to Ma when she wanted me to learn. I need to know how to read a newspaper and know about what's happenin'." Her words tumbled out as she became more eager to explain her feelings. "Or read a letter meant for me my own self! Or, most of all, write down my own thinkin'!" She lifted his hand in hers. "Oh Josh, learn me to read and write. Please!"

"Course I will, Nan, what all I can."

"Can we start tomorrow?" she asked.

"The town of Sut, Sut," Nancy stumbled over the letters.

"Sutton," Josh said softly.

"Sutton," Nancy repeated, "was over...rid...den," she continued slowly, "by 1-3-5 Confederates." She smiled proudly as she unhesitatingly pronounced Confederates. Josh and Nancy sat at the table, a newpaper spread out before them. Josh moved his finger along, pointing at the letters as Nancy slowly pronounced them.

Alice and Luke tried to act disinterested at Nancy's stumbling efforts to put meaning to the words. Finally Alice burst out impatiently. "Oh, for pity's sake, do get to the rest of the story."

"I'm a readin', Alice. I'm readin'. So far this is as fast as I kin get."

"Yer doin' good, too," Luke chimed in. "But we want to know what the newspaper says happened over to Braxton County. I only heard scraps of it. This is serious business. Go on, Josh. You read it out to us."

With an apologetic look, Josh lifted the newspaper and began to read. "On the twenty-ninth of December, the town of Sutton, in central Braxton County, was overridden by 135 Confederates, who proceeded to set fire and burn many of the prominent homes and buildings. The following day, a troop, hastily mustered, of 400 Federal soldiers, marched into Webster County in pursuit of those Rebels who had torched Sutton. They overtook the savage enemy at the town of Glades and in the ensuing fight, 22 Confederates were killed and 29 houses of suspected Rebel bushwhackers were burned in retribution."

"Savage!" Nancy jumped to her feet. "They call the Rebels savage. What about the Federals burnin' 29 families outa their homes!"

"Both sides is savage," Alice muttered. "This here fightin' in the hills is more than jist the big war between the states. It's neighbor and kin—one aginst t'other. Tain't clear no more who's on what side. Houses burnt to jist the chimney left standin', families with young'uns scattered inta the hills. Tain't fitten action fer God-fearin' people." Alice leaned back in her chair, hands spread open on her lap. Shaking her head slowly from side to side, she repeated almost to herself, "It ain't fitten'."

After a few moments, Josh spoke up again. "Do you want me to keep readin'? The newspaper has more to say 'bout President Lincoln and what's goin' on in Washington."

"Huh, Lincoln," Nancy snorted as she sat down. "Some folks call him the great ape."

"Go on, Josh," Luke said. "Read us some more."

"It is the opinion of this editor that the Army of the Potomac has been inactive in the defense of Washington long enough. The ignominious defeat of the Federal troops at Ball's Bluff, Virginia has gone unavenged too long. Though General McClellan lies incapacitated at the present time with typhoid fever, his long inaction cannot be attributed to this alone. Not only must pressure be brought to bear upon Richmond, the capital of the Confederacy, but Federal control must be maintained over not only western Virginia, but also the disputed border states of Kentucky and Missouri."

"Kentucky," Nancy murmured. "I hope Mary and the young'uns is safe."

Josh continued, "Frustration at the inactivity of the Army of the Potomac has reached high levels. President Lincoln himself has been heard to say, 'If General McClellan does not wish to use the army, I should like to borrow it, provided it can be made to do something.'"

They smiled at the quote. "Seems like the 'great ape' has a wit about him," Josh said.

"And the Federal army has its own problems," Luke added.

The winter passed quietly in the small cabin tucked into the hills of Calhoun County. Snows blew fiercely across the rocks and mountains and filled the valleys, making any kind of travel difficult and opportunities for raids by the Moccasin Rangers next to impossible. There were a few messages relayed from Captain Conley by the occasional lone hunter, and Josh made a weekly trek to his family's farm for newspapers, supplies, and word of any local gossip. Nancy had always been quick to learn the activities of hunting, riding, or shooting, but never before had she hungered for what she called book learnin'. Now she reached for the newspaper, already weeks old by the time Josh returned with it, and immediately began to read it aloud. And when there were no newspapers handy, she studied the tattered pages of Alice's family Bible. Less and less did Josh have to prompt her with a word, although sometimes she hesitated to admit she did not understand the meanings. "Soon you'll be teachin' me, Nan," Josh said once, almost forlornly.

When she wasn't studying, Nancy was busy with Alice, stitching the intricate pattern of her quilt or grinding the dried yarrow, mullein, and burdock roots with the pestle and mortar. "This here's what makes a good poultice for a wound," Alice said.

"Things is so quiet now, it don't seem like we'll be needin' to patch up wounds," Nancy replied. "I wish it could stay like this."

"Huh, if wishes was horses, beggars would ride," Alice said. She pounded harder with the wooden pestle.

When the small cabin walls became too confining, Nancy spent hours in the barn with Lady. The horse would nuzzle Nancy's shoulder as she brushed her silky coat. "Soon the spring thaw will be here, and you and me can ride up and down the holler agin, Lady."

"You can't go ridin' through the holler awhile yet, Nan," Josh spoke as he entered the barn, leading his horse. "Yer famous now," he said as he pulled a newspaper from his coat pocket and handed it to her. "Here, read about yerself."

"Read about me?" Nancy looked at the page that was folded over and creased around a small article. She stared with amazement at the letters, which spelled out her name for all to see in the newspaper. Slowly she read aloud. "A liberal reward is offered for information leading to the whereabouts and eventual capture of a Miss Nancy Hart, about 16 years of age, black hair, dark eyes, fair complexion, considered to be comely in appearance, and known to be a Rebel guide and spy. She has been reported in the company of known Confederate guerilla, Perry Conley, for whom a death warrant has been posted by the United States government. Contact Provost Marshall Office, Braxton County."

Nancy flopped down on a bale of hay, mouth open, the newspaper at her feet. Josh went to her. He gently took her hands in his. "Don't fret, Nan. Yer safe here with us. Ain't a body knows yer here 'cept my folks, and they sure won't say nothin'."

"Oh, Josh," she whispered.

"Soon as the thaw comes and the trails are passable, we'll be up in the caves again, and you'll be safe."

"It ain't gonna be over so quick if you listen to Luke and Alice." She lowered her head and whispered, "I'm a wanted spy."

Josh placed his hand under her chin and lifted her face to his own. "You ain't no such thing," he said. "No more'n the rest of us, fightin' to protect our rights. When this fight is finished," he placed his hands on her shoulders and pulled her to him. "When this fight is finished," he repeated, "I want you to be my wife."

"Oh Josh, I can't," Nancy began to protest.

"Don't say nothin' yet," he spoke softly into her hair as he stroked her back. "It's jist that I got a patch of land from my pa, up yonder near my special place. I'll build you a cabin, not small like this, but a right nice size with a chimney at both ends so that," he lowered his voice, "so that when young'uns come, we'll have room to spare."

Nancy did not know what to say. Her head swam with images, Mary, the young'uns, the captain so tall and commanding, spy, wanted...she was a wanted spy. She closed her eyes and breathed in the scent of Lady, the hay, the leather tack hanging on the barn wall, but most of all the scent of Josh, his hair, his skin, the cloth of his coat. It all felt so familiar and safe. One word crept into her brain and twisted itself around until it was all she could think of—spy.

Chapter Thirteen

Patches of earth appeared as the snows of winter melted, swelling the rivers and streams. Witch Hazel poked its yellow head up, the first sign of spring after the long winter. "Alice says she's a stayin' here, Luke. She won't come up inta the hills with us." Nancy spoke as Luke skinned a deer which hung on the outside barn wall by its hind feet. His sharp knife shone in the sunlight as he deftly pulled and cut away the deerskin hide. The pink meat of the stripped animal quivered wet and glistening as Luke pulled.

"Ain't no use in abandonin' the place. A body's got to be here workin' the fields or the Federals'll mark us for secesh. We don't need no barn burnin' here."

"Maybe I should stay with Alice."

In exasperation Luke stabbed the knife deep into the soft flesh of the animal. Then he turned to Nancy, "You can't stay here, girl. Don't you know yer wanted? Now that the snow's meltin', the Federals will be millin' 'round here like fleas on a dog."

"But, Luke, Alice will be alone," Nancy started.

"Don't you know I been thinkin' on that. I'll be comin' back here regular to help Alice with the plantin' and to show there's a man about the place." He turned and pulled the knife from the deer carcass. It made a dull sucking sound.

Nancy walked to the cabin to help Alice prepare the evening meal. She and Josh and Luke planned to leave at dawn to meet the captain and the other rangers in the mountain caves.

Even though the snow was melted, except for patches here and there on the north sides of the rocks and trees, the dawn seemed as cold and desolate as if it were still the dead of winter. Nancy, dressed in her men's britches and with a new deerskin jacket Alice had stitched for her, stood just outside the cabin door. Her hair, which had been cut to shoulder length, was pulled back tightly under a wide-brimmed hat just like the one Josh wore.

"There now, child," Alice spoke firmly, reaching for Nancy's hands, "you look like a young fella'. Maybe not as tall nor broad as the likes of Josh, but still a strong 'n able one. You mind you keep that hair of yourn pulled back and hid. I should've cut it shorter so'n there'd be no question, but I jist couldn't bring myself to cut all that black glory. And," Alice leaned in closer to whisper, "you mind you keep yer bosom wrapped good 'n tight when you're ridin' in them raids so's there's no raisin' a question you're a woman. Last year it might not've been noticed, but you done some fillin' out o'er this long winter."

Nancy nodded. She felt her eyes brim up with tears and tried to hold them back. Alice's hand felt cold and bony in her own. It was hard to leave this woman who so seldom showed the emotion she was showing now, but who, Nancy somehow knew, loved her more dearly than her own mother ever had.

Alice continued, "It's different now, child, you know. It's no longer for the fun or adventure. You're ridin' with the rangers for yer life and you play the part no matter what. Now, you get on afore the sun comes slippin' o'er them hills."

Nancy nodded again. She didn't trust her voice, but quickly hugged Alice's bony frame to her and brushed her lips across her cheek. Then she was climbing up on Lady while Josh, already mounted on his own horse, held her reins. They started slowly away while Luke and Alice said their good-byes. Nancy turned once to see them with their arms about each other.

As they travelled up toward the caves, Nancy realized that this time she did not go with a sense of excitement or anticipation as she first had last summer. Her anger at the Federals was even greater now after what they had done to Will and now that the Home Guard was forcing its ways on all the western Virginians. But along with that anger was mixed a fear and dread, which was new to her. A fear of what those blue-coated Federals could do because of their sheer numbers.

Spring was starting with its hints of green, especially in the lush grass growing along the banks of the fast-running creeks, but the leaves were just budding and did not yet offer the cover the rangers needed to travel under. Nancy worried that they had not waited long enough. During the winter, she had looked long and hard at the rugged mountains with all their humps and dips and spiney ridges clearly defined by the white of the snow and the starkness of the bare trees. No one, not man nor animal, could travel undetected by the bare eye. Even when the snow melted and the ground was the same dull brown color as the tree trunks, any unusual movement could be seen from the floor of the valley. The Home Guard had used that visibility very clearly during the winter to make both their presence and strength known.

"Where'd that little rascal come from?" Josh asked as they came into camp. A young child with bright red curly hair ran straight at Nancy, waving a stick. Lady snorted and danced sideways. Nancy pulled the horse up and quickly dismounted. She caught the squealing, kicking boy around the middle with one arm and held Lady's reins with the other as a girl about her own age came running toward them, her chestnut hair bouncing over her shoulders.

"Thank you, mister," she said as she retrieved the wriggling child. "He's a real scalawag! Daniel Hiram Carpenter, you stop your running around and bothering this man!"

Mister? At first Nancy was surprised at the mistake, but then she smiled. *The disguise worked.* Josh had ridden off to join the other rangers, and Nancy found herself alone to deal with this girl and the unhappy child, who was screaming to be put down.

"All right, but you quieten down now and keep in plain sight or the captain won't let us stay. You hear, Daniel?" As soon as his feet touched the ground, Daniel was off running as fast as his little legs could carry him. The girl sighed and shook her head. "I'm Becky Carpenter from over to Webster County. The Federals burned us out, and the captain was kind enough to let us take shelter up here, but I believe we've about worn out our welcome." Her freckled complexion colored slightly as her green eyes met Nancy's steady gaze.

"Jist hold on a minute," Nancy said. " I ain't no mister. I go by the name of Nancy Hart." She pulled off the slouch hat and shook her hair out about her collar.

Becky looked at her in surprise. "I'm sorry. I thought sure you was a fella'—maybe a bit puny, but still...Nancy Hart...why I heard tell of you...riding with the rangers and dressed as a boy. Ain't you skairt? They got a price on your head, you know?"

Before Nancy could answer, Becky continued. "I must say you look better than I thought you would, cuttin' your hair off like that. I wouldn't be caught dead in them clothes and..."

Nancy cut her short. "I got to see to my horse now, and you best see to little Daniel yonder." Nancy nodded her head toward the boy who was running recklessly close to the rope corral and the feet of the horses.

It seemed Becky Carpenter never stopped talking. That night around the small campfire she was still telling her story. "Since Joseph joined up with the Federals, my pa says he's got no son by that name. That's when Mama took sick, and she's been poorly ever since. I sure don't know what's gonna befall us." Becky turned her green eyes on Josh.

Nancy stood and threw the remainder of her coffee sputtering into the fire. She walked away into the shadows, still hearing Becky's voice chirping on and on. A few moments later Josh came up behind her. "I sure don't know what's gonna befall us," Nancy imitated Becky's sweet voice. "How did you contrive to tear yourself away from those big, wide eyes?"

"Oh, Nan," Josh put his arm around her shoulders and pulled her close. "She's jist a silly girl. You know that. But it seems the captain realizes his mistake in bringin' the family up here. He's arranged to get them out tomorra'. They're takin' the wife and little Daniel down to her kin in Greenbrier Valley, and Becky's goin' to her granny's. The old lady needs help on her clearin' in Nicholas County. Her pa's been too good to the rangers, not to look out for 'em."

"Nicholas County! That's too close! Becky don't know how to keep her mouth shut. She'll have every Home Guard in three counties up here afore you know it, and that'll be the end of all of us."

"Don't go gettin' riled up," Josh said in his calming voice. "Becky ain't like you with a horse and gun and followin' trails. We'll take her up and down so many ridges and into so many hollers, by the time she gets to her granny's, she'll think the sun rises in the north and sets in the south."

"Well, it can't be too soon for me. Do you know, she done set up her bed right next to mine in the womanfolk's corner of the cave. Why, I wager she talks in her sleep all through the night! Oh, Lord, I miss Alice."

A thick fog hung over the mountain the next morning, and for once Nancy hoped it would not burn off too quickly. The heavy cloud seemed to muffle everything, including Becky's voice. Finally the Carpenters' meager household goods were bundled up. Hiram Carpenter effortlessly lifted his frail wife to the saddle on a small, sturdy mare. He wrapped a smoke-stained coverlet about her shoulders and swung himself up behind her. Nancy noticed that the woman never focused her dark circled eyes on anyone, but had a perpetually bewildered look on her pale, sunken face. "There now, Martha darlin', you jist hang onta Nellie and we'll git you down the mountain." Hiram Carpenter encircled his wife with his arms and lifted the reins.

While Hiram was getting his wife settled, Becky had appeared in a blue wool cloak and bonnet as if going off to town for a visit, and Nancy felt a twinge of envy. She had never owned a dress quite that fine. Calico was the best she'd ever had, and now she looked down at her rough, homespun trousers. Becky held her little brother tightly by the hand and said, "Now you just ride with me and no squirmin', you hear, Daniel?" He was bundled so tightly in a jacket and muffler that only his little nose peaked out the top. Nancy wondered how long it would be until he squirmed out of that.

"Allow me, Miss Becky." The captain placed his powerful hands about Becky's waist and lifted her up on the saddled horse.

"Thank you kindly, Captain." She flashed her dimpled smile, her eyes darting around to make sure everyone noticed who had helped her mount. "My family's much obliged for your hospitality during our misfortune."

"Our pleasure, Miss Becky," the captain answered as he deftly reached around to grab Daniel as he went to crawl beneath the horse. "Now you hold tight to this young'un," he said as he lifted the little bundle and placed him in front of Becky. "Here's something sweet for you to chew on." He placed a sassafras root in the little boy's hand. Big round eyes stared out at this giant of a man. For once in his young life, Daniel remained motionless. "It'll keep him quiet on the long ride."

Becky took a deep breath and sighed. The captain shook hands with Hiram and stepped back as the Carpenter family, escorted by Josh and Luke, rode out of camp. Becky turned to wave and called out, "You come pay me a visit at my granny's, Nancy."

Nancy nodded, but did not return the wave until she saw Josh raise his hand to her. Then, reluctantly, she raised her hand. The camp seemed unnaturally quiet and deserted after the group left. Nancy felt at a loss of what to do. There weren't even any household chores to be done, other than gathering firewood. If she were home with Alice, she could be quilting or pouring over a newspaper.

Within a week or two, spring seemed to burst out all over. One day the leaves were still in bud and the next the trees were in full leaf, casting shadows and shade across the forest. The sweet smell of service trees filled the woods, followed by the lacey white of the dogwoods and the delicate redbuds. Nancy longed to be walking behind old Jeremiah, plowing her family's cornfield. *Did Pa sell old Jeremiah when they went back to Tazewell?* Nancy wondered. *Even bendin' over the rows of Ma's garden, plantin' beans would be good, feelin' the warm sun on my back.*

"The meadows'll soon be blowzin' with all kind of color," she said to Josh as they leaned back against a rock, warm from the sun, and looked out at the valley.

"Yeah, and the hills'll soon be growin' with all kind of Home Guard and Federals, too. Ain't no time to be payin' a visit, Nan, even a night time one."

"Can you always read my mind, Josh? Or is it jist when we're here in your special place?" Nancy sighed and Josh wrapped his arms around her, pulling her closer.

Each time Luke returned from his journey down to the cabin, Nancy was waiting to ask, "How is Alice fairin'?"

"Fair to middlin'," he'd reply without fail, but this last time, along with a packet of newspapers, he handed Nancy a neatly folded bundle.

"Oh," she gasped. "My quilt! Alice finished my quilt!" Carefully she spread it open across a boulder and slowly traced the wedding ring pattern with her finger, noticing Alice's tiny, even stitches. "Alice has been right busy to get all this done," she said softly. "I'll be takin' right good care of this."

As spring unfolded its thick green canopy over the ridges and hollows, the Moccasin Rangers resumed their raids. They struck swiftly and often, covering distances quickly and inflicting damage on the enemy encampments and outposts with little damage to themselves. One raid became like another, until the weather turned from springlike warmth to the heat of summer. Always after each raid, the mocking laughter rang through the hills. The newspapers called it "ghostly laughter which strikes fear into the hearts of all who hear it." Nancy found the idea of the Moccasin Rangers being ghostly very funny. *Some "ghosts," sittin' 'round the campfire of an evenin' drinkin' from a jug, spittin' tobacco, and scratchin' theirselves. Ain't never seen no ghost do that.* She laughed as she read the newspaper account aloud to a group of the rangers.

It was mid-June. Nancy stifled a yawn as she rode behind Josh in the midst of the rangers. All she could think of was stretching out on her quilt in the corner of the cave and sleeping and sleeping. It seemed they had been out every night lately, and this particular raid had taken them deep into Webster County. They still had a long ride ahead of them, but the captain had laughed and boasted it had been one of their best. Hadn't they gotten six new horses to be sent on to the Confederate lines?

One of our best? Nancy asked herself. *I no longer know one from t'other and it still don't seem we're makin' headway agin' the Federals.*

"Nan! Pull up!" Josh hissed at her. Nancy sat up straighter, reining Lady in and brought her mind back to the present.

"What...," she started to say, but suddenly all was confusion. A shot was fired; then a rapid succession of others. There were blue bellies everywhere, not just in front. They must have come upon a whole contingent resting in the woods! Nancy wheeled Lady around, at the same time reaching for her carbine in the socket at her side. More shots, and she saw the captain fall off his horse. The large chestnut reared up on its hind legs and down again, its hooves just missing the captain. Josh hissed at her again, "This way!" Still she had not fired a shot, but was frantically trying to take aim at the Federal drawing close to the captain on the ground. She could see the captain pushing himself up and grabbing for his rifle. He fired and fired again. A shot came from behind Nancy, and the blue belly near the captain fell. Nancy turned around and saw that it was Josh who had fired. He grabbed Lady's bridle and was pulling her away, deeper into the woods.

"But the capt...," Nancy was saying, and she turned around to see him on his feet now like a huge wounded bear, one leg dragging. He swung his rifle like a club at the men surrounding him on horseback. And then one struck down on the captain's head with the butt of his rifle as another shot was fired. The captain fell just as the man, who had swung the blow, fell from his horse.

The smoke was heavy and close, and Nancy's eyes were burning. *No! No!* She screamed in her mind. But now the blue bellies were after her and Josh, and they were racing through the dense trees and underbrush, branches whipping across her shoulders and flicking against her cheeks. No time to turn and fight—only to ride frantically any direction they could manage—Josh just behind her, sheltering her from gunshots. No time to think, to let her mind register what had happened—only to travel up and up. Finally, she realized there were no more pounding hooves behind them, no more shots being fired—only their own noises, their own frantic hearts pounding, the ragged breathing of their own horses.

"Josh," Nancy called back, "can we stop? Can we..."

"No, Nan," he said, his voice weak from exertion. "Keep on jist a little farther...we gotta be sure...jist a little farther."

Gradually they slowed. The horses could be pushed no longer. And the silence settled around them. They were all alone. Nancy's heart was still pounding, her mouth dry and her face streaming with sweat. She had lost her hat to one of the branches, and hair clung to her forehead and across her eyes. For the first time she turned to look at Josh, the terror of seeing the captain clubbed down still in her mind. Josh was white, as white as his hair plastered on his face, and he looked like he couldn't catch his breath.

"Josh," Nancy said, her voice barely a squeak. She leaned in close to him, and it was then she saw his arm clutched close about his midsection. Blood was seeping out around his sleeve and across the front of his shirt. "You're hurt!" Instantly she jumped off Lady and reached for Josh.

"Easy, Nan, jist slow," he managed to say. "Ease me down real slow."

As gently as she could, she held him, trying to support his weight as he slid down from his horse. He groaned and bit into his lip as he slumped to his knees, then all the way to the ground. His face was so white, even his light eyes looked coal dark in his face, and dirt-streaked sweat glistened across his forehead. Nancy eased him on to his back in a bed of moss behind a large boulder. He lay silent for a time, his eyes closed while Nancy straightened his legs out and then pulled his torn shirt away from his ribs. The bullet seemed to have just grazed his midsection. There was no gaping wound, only a raised hump as if his rib bones had been broken, and it was already showing a large bruise. As she pulled his sleeve away, fresh blood flowed, and then she saw the gash in his arm.

Oh, Lord Almighty!...Stay calm...What would Alice do?...Stop the blood. That's the first thing. Nancy took what was left of Josh's shirt, tore it, and tied a piece securely around his arm. She needed more binding and for once wished she had a handy petticoat. *Binding,* she thought again. Quickly she removed her shirt and released the long strip of cotton Alice had given her to bind her bosom. Donning her shirt again, she knelt close and wiped her hand gently across his forehead, clearing the hair and sweat from his eyes. "Josh, can you hear me?" He made a noise, barely moving his lips and not opening his eyes. "Can you hear me?" she asked again. This time he made another sound and opened his eyes, giving a slight nod. "Good. I'm gonna sit you up. I gotta strap your ribs, get 'em back in place so they can mend."

She crawled behind him, pushing his back up and holding him as straight as she could. He groaned, sweat pouring down his face. "I'm sorry, Josh, so sorry," Nancy murmured. "I don't want to hurt you any more'n I have to."

"I know," he whispered. "Jist get it done."

When he was in a sitting position, she reached for the long strip and began to wrap, pressing firmly down on the strange hump that bulged at his rib. She kept wrapping tightly in spite of his moans, working as quickly as she could. She tied the end into place and laid him back down. His arm was bleeding again. "Now, don't move. I'm goin' to look for some yarrow to staunch the blood." She rose to go, but immediately knelt back down and pressed her lips to his forehead. "I'll be right back, Josh. Only a minute." His lips parted in the faintest smile.

It seemed to Nancy that it took a long time—much too long—to find a small, sunny clearing with the pungent yarrow blooming. She plucked handfuls of the yellow blossoming clusters, and, not knowing how else to carry them back to where Josh lay, thrust the blooms inside the front of her shirt. She allowed Lady to quench her thirst from a small stream and drank some herself; then splashed the cold water on her face. *I gotta remember to get Josh's horse, Red, to some water, too. These two animals have been run hard.* The image of the falling captain reared again in her mind. *No, I can't think of that now. Not now.* And she hurried back to Josh, who lay just as still and as white as when she left him. Gently she dressed his wound with the yarrow flowers while Josh winced silently.

"Nan," he whispered, "you gotta scout around, see where we are. Maybe find a place to harbor us a few days. Don't think I can move too far."

"I know, Josh. I already thought of that. We're near the river—the Gauley with its big carved-out canyon. I caught sight of it when I found the yarrow. Accordin' to my reckonin', we're inta Nicholas County and not too far from that Becky Carpenter's granny's place. I'm gonna have to leave you again, but I'll be back soon." This time before she left, she tied Red loosely to a nearby tree within sight of Josh, so the horse could easily feed on the lush grass. Then she took the blanket roll from behind his saddle and gently covered Josh. "So you don't take cold," she said and again leaned down to kiss his forehead. "One more thing, Josh. I'm loadin' yer carbine and layin' it here next to your right arm...in case you need it." She touched his cheek lightly with her fingertips and then left.

It had to be nearly noon by now. The sun was hot and high overhead when she reached the clearing and looked down the hollow toward the little cabin. It was neatly kept with a front porch and rocker. Larger than Alice's and Luke's place. *Luke! I ain't even had time to think of Luke and what became of him! Did he get away? No...not now. I can't think of that now.* But for the thin line of smoke coming from the chimney, it could have been abandoned. Nancy stood there a few minutes longer and then the door opened and Becky, *yes it had to be Becky with that walk and that chestnut-colored hair,* came into the yard with a bucket for spring water. Nancy didn't waste any more time.

Chapter Fourteen

Urging Lady forward, she picked her way down the steep slope. "I know, girl, you had a hard day. You'll be able to rest soon." She stroked her neck as they moved. Becky had disappeared into the springhouse, but two hounds came bounding out from behind the cabin, barking and growling. Lady moved skittishly. She was not used to dogs. The captain had not allowed them in the rangers' camp. "Barking'll draw the blue bellies," he had said. Nancy started to dismount, but one dog jumped up, yapping at her leg. Just then the old lady cracked the door open, and Becky came out of the springhouse carrying the heavy bucket.

"Elmer, George! What's that racket?" Becky called out, and then she recognized Nancy. "Good Lord, Nancy Hart! You do look a sight! What brings you here? Elmer, George, you get on over here, right now, do you hear?"

The dogs quieted, sniffing around the ground and at Nancy's feet as she dismounted. Then, losing interest, they wandered back to the cabin and crawled into the cool shade beneath the porch.

All the while Becky had rambled on. "Granny, this here's the Nancy Hart I told you 'bout. See? She's wearin' men's britches, and you do look a sight, Nancy. Your face is scratched and your shirt is torn—"

"Hush up, girl," her granny interrupted. "Give her a chance to talk." She took Nancy by the hand, pulling her toward the house.

After hearing Nancy's story, Becky for once was wide-eyed and speechless. Tears welled up in her eyes. "Killed?...The captain is...dead?"

Nancy nodded briskly, willing herself not to think too hard about it.

"Why, Granny, we gotta help these folks. They helped Ma and Pa and me when we needed it. Fair's fair."

"I ain't hidin' no wounded ranger in my home. This place is all I got, and if'n I was discovered to be shelterin', they'd burn me out jist as they did yer pa. You take yer friend up the holler behind the spring. There's a cave there safe and dry, and if the Federals come 'round, they won't see no trace of them."

"Thank you kindly, Miz Carpenter," Nancy said. She was starting to feel so tired now, so exhausted, but she knew she had to get back to Josh.

When Nancy returned, for an instant she thought Josh had died. His pale skin was almost waxlike, but then his eyelashes flickered. She knelt down close to him, whispering, afraid that if she spoke too loudly it would cause him more pain. "Josh, sweet Josh, I'm back."

He opened his eyes and again the faint smile was on his lips.

"I brought you some water, and then I gotta get you moved. Can you do it?"

"I can with your help." He spoke slowly, each word a painful effort. With Nancy's support he struggled to his feet. Then came the painful task of mounting Red. The effort was so great that he nearly fainted.

"I'll hold you in place," Nancy said. Quickly she took Lady's reins and slipped them over the horn of Red's saddle. Then she climbed up behind Josh. His bulk and weight were greater than she had imagined. He slipped sideways, nearly falling several times on their journey. Nancy clung to him and winced with each moan and cry that he uttered. She was grateful when finally he slumped forward, unconscious, his head upon Red's neck.

"I hope the trail wasn't too much for him," Nancy said to Becky as the two girls half carried, half dragged Josh into the tiny cave, nestled in the hollow. It wasn't like the big cavern the rangers had used, where the smoke from their fire and torches could find its way up into the cavernous ceiling or back through the passages and crevices and not smother them. A cookfire in this one with its low ceiling would smoke them out. Nancy knew she'd only be able to build a fire at night just outside the entrance. At least there was dense underbrush, and she'd have to be careful not to wear a clear trail.

Becky, for all her yammering and chatter, was a good worker. She quickly laid a wool blanket over clean straw and had a bucket of spring water already there. "We'll put him here, and he'll be good as new soon," she said. "Granny jist made a pot of chicken and dumplin's. I'll bring some to you directly. Oh, and a dress for yerself, too. It might be a bit slack on you, but it'll do. Granny says if your gonna be seen about the place, you gotta look like a respectable visitin' relation." Becky paused long enough to catch her breath. Then, looking directly at Nancy, continued. "And I best bring some lye soap, too. I know you ain't had a look at yourself, but you could use a good scrubbin' down at the creek."

In the quiet that followed, Nancy could hear nothing but Josh's labored breathing. The wound in Josh's arm showed fresh blood on the bandage. "Blazes, I'd best bind that up agin," she said. Josh did not respond. Nancy used a fresh cloth Becky had left and some of the cool, clear water to cleanse his face and to wash around the wound. Josh still did not move.

"Josh, sweet Josh, don't you go and die on me. You're all I got. Don't even know if Luke's dead or alive nor how Alice is fairin'," she whispered as she leaned over him. "Sides, I'd miss you."

Josh opened his eyes and focused on Nancy for a moment, a faint smile played around the corners of his mouth. A whisper of a moan was all he could manage, but it was enough for Nancy. She lay next to him, resting her head on his shoulder and cried.

During the next few days Josh took a fever and drifted in and out of consciousness. Nancy did not leave his side, wiping his brow when he grew feverish. His chills seemed to worsen when the sun went down. She pulled the blanket around them and held herself close against him through the long night, sharing her body warmth.

On the third morning, she woke to find Josh looking at her, his eyes wide and clear. "Mornin', Nan," he said.

"Josh!" Nancy sat up. "You're awake and you're cool," she said as she placed her hand against his cheek. She scrambled to her feet.

He tried to raise himself up, but from the pained look on his face, it was clear he had forgotten about his ribs. "No need to move away so fast. I'm still pretty sick, you know." He smiled.

Nancy, wearing only the shift that Becky had provided, pulled the calico dress over her head. "I'll see to yer breakfast, Josh. I reckon you're hungry and need some food." Her cheeks were burning red, and Josh would not stop gazing at her.

"Nan," he said quietly. Then again more softly, "Nan, you're beautiful."

"I'll be back directly," she said as she hurried out of the cave and ran toward the cabin.

Josh grew stronger daily and gradually was able to move around slowly and stiffly, though he didn't dare go beyond the underbrush outside the cave during daylight. Nancy spent more time about the fields helping Becky with the garden. It felt good to be out in the sunlight again, but Nancy glanced often toward the hollow, knowing Josh was there waiting, perhaps even watching her through the cover of leaves.

During the cooler morning hours, they gathered vegetables and pulled weeds in the garden. Through the hot afternoons, the girls would often sit in the shade of the porch to thread beans on long strings and lay them out flat on the floor.

"Directly you can hang these from the rafters in the barn to dry," Granny said from the door.

"I'm not one for climbin' ladders, Nancy. I'm sure glad of your help," Becky said.

Nancy sighed and continued threading beans. "It's the least I can do," she replied.

"Tomorra' is market day. I'm gonna hitch up Granny's cart and go inta town. You want to come along?"

Nancy sat forward and dropped the beans into her lap. "It'd pleasure me to do that, but I reckon I best stay hid," she replied. "Could you get a newspaper? And keep your ears open for talk of the Moccasin Rangers. But remember, Becky, don't say nothin' bout me and Josh."

"Nancy Hart," Becky said with a hurt look on her face, "I allow I'm a might chatty, but I'm not daft nor weak in the head. I know better than to speak your name or Josh's."

Nancy tried to make amends. "I know that, Becky, and you and yer granny are good to us. It's jist that I guess I'm a bit...scared after all that's happened."

Becky reached over and touched Nancy's arm. "I'll get a newspaper, and maybe I can get us a *Godey's Lady's Book.* I do like to look at all those pretty dress pictures." Nancy smiled and shook her head.

Josh was feeling better. Now when Nancy returned to the cave, instead of finding him asleep or sitting quietly at the entrance, he was pacing back and forth impatiently. "Here's some fried chicken and apple cider Granny sent for our supper." She placed the jug and basket of chicken on the ground next to him.

"Nan, I ain't hungry. I can't abide jist sittin' here whilst you do everthin'."

"I know, Josh, but you ain't all healed yet, at least not fit to ride, so's you best eat." She sat next to him and began to munch on some chicken from the basket.

"What's become of the others, Nan? How are we gonna know?"

"Becky's gone to town, and she said she'd bring back a newspaper and be listenin' for talk of the rangers. Josh, I know what we seen, but I still can't believe that a body as powerful and as shinin' as Perry Conley could be snuffed out so quick!"

Josh placed his good arm around her and pulled her close. "It don't matter how bright the sun shines, Nan, the dark still comes."

It was dark now, and Nancy could see through the trees a light in the window of the cabin. She bent to make a small fire just outside the cave. She longed for the solid walls of a cabin and the warmth of food cooked on a stove or even a blazing hearthfire.

Josh covered her hand with his. "Never mind, Nan. Soon we'll be married and we'll be finished with camp-fires. We'll have our own hearthfire for you to cook on and a soft feather bed for us to sleep on." Josh stopped, suddenly shy. "You will marry me, won't you Nan? I love you, and I want you for my wife."

Nancy rose and faced him. Slipping her arms around his neck, she turned her face up to him.

"I love you, Josh, and I'll be right proud to be Mistress Joshua Douglas."

He bent to kiss her.

"Yoohoo," Becky trilled in her high voice. "I got you a newspaper, and more."

"It's a good thing we're not tryin' to be quiet up here," Nancy said to Josh under her breath.

Becky picked her way through the underbrush and came close to the fire, waving a newspaper in the air. "I even brought you some candles so's you can read all night if you've a mind to."

Josh eagerly took the paper. "Thank you kindly, Miss Becky. Is there any word of the rangers?" he asked.

"Well now, I was comin' to that," she said and stepped aside as Luke came forward into the light of the fire. "I brought you a special package from town," Becky added.

"Luke!" Before he could even say a word, Nancy had her arms around him. "How's Alice? Is everthin' all right at home? How'd you get away from the ambush?"

"Hold on, girl. Hold on." Luke extended his hand to Josh. "Good to see you, son. How bad is it?" He nodded his head toward Josh's wounded arm.

"I'll be fine, thanks to Nan," Josh replied. Becky cleared her throat. "Oh, and Miss Becky and her granny, of course."

I'll go on back down to Granny now," Becky said. "Nancy, I'll see you in the morning."

They sat in the small cave, talking by candlelight and making plans. "The Moccasin Rangers is disbanded," Luke told them. "Some is gone south to join up, but most is gone to Captain George Downs' Company A, 19th Virginia Cavalry. It's all Moccasin Rangers, but it's guaranteed that the enlistment papers is dated July 1861, so's a body can't prove any of the unit was with the rangers. No sir, guaranteed, that when the rangers was raidin', our boys was in the Confederate army."

When Luke finished speaking, Nancy and Josh looked at each other. "I'll have to go, Nan, soon as I'm fit." She nodded and lowered her head.

"When does the itinerant preacher ride through here?" Nancy spoke as she poured corn upon a large flat stone while Becky rolled a smaller, rounded stone back and forth to crush the kernels. Becky stopped pushing the stone and stood upright. "Why do you want to know that? It's the first time I heard you talk 'bout preachin'?" Narrowing her eyes, she peered into Nancy's face. "You're not fixin'..." Then eyes wide, "You are! You and Josh are fixin' to marry!" she squealed. Grabbing Nancy around the middle, she spun them both around and around, squealing all the while. "Shhh, stop Becky," Nancy said, trying to stop the dizzying swing, but in spite of herself, she had to laugh. When her head finally stopped spinning and she went to pick up the crushing stone again, a flash of blue caught her eye. She gasped, grabbing Becky's wrist. At the far end of the long field were five blue-coated Federals, headed straight toward them. For an instant she froze. All the terror of the ambush rushed back. By this time Becky, too, saw them, and together, without speaking, they raced for the cabin, bolting the door behind them.

"You two sit over yonder on the bed and don't make a sound," Granny said.

Heavy footsteps crossed the porch, and then there was pounding on the door. "Hello the house. Is anyone there?"

"Can't you see the smoke arisin' from my chimney. Course I'm here," Granny responded. "What do you want?"

"Lt. Col. William Starr of the the 9th West Virginia, ma'am. My men and I are procuring provisions, ma'am. We'd like to pay you or trade. Can you open the door?"

"I ain't openin' and I ain't got nothin' to trade."

"We'd like fresh eggs, butter, vegetables from your garden, ma'am. We've got sugar loaves to trade." Granny did not respond. "We've got salt."

Granny lifted her hand to the latch. "No, don't," Nancy whispered.

"Hush. Salt is dear and hard to come by," she whispered to Nancy. The old woman opened the door a crack. "You got salt?" she asked.

"Yes, ma'am," the colonel replied. "Kerner, Davis, bring those bags of salt over here. You two orderlies, take those empty sacks and fill them from the garden

with beans and corn and such that will make a fair trade."
Then without hesitation, he pushed the door wide and
entered the room. "Lt. Col. William Starr, ma'am," he
repeated and removed his hat, placing it under his arm.
"Afternoon ladies." His sword clinked against the kitchen
table as he moved toward the corner where Nancy and
Becky sat. "No need to be frightened. We mean you no
harm."

Nancy kept her head averted. To keep her hands
occupied, she had taken up Granny's discarded mending
and now tried to push the darning needle through the
wool cloth with shaking fingers.

The two other men entered the cabin now, each with
a bag of salt, and laid them on the table. "I hope forty
pounds is satisfactory, ma'am," he said. Granny nodded
silently and walked toward the table to finger the bags.
"You keep a right nice looking garden, ma'am. Your men
folk about the place?"

"Ain't got no men folk," Granny mumbled. "All gone
off to war. Only woman folk to tend the place."

"These two young ladies must be a great help to you
then, ma'am. Are they relations?"

"Granddaughters," she mumbled.

Colonel Starr stretched his hand out to Becky, who
hesitantly took it. "Pleased to make your acquaintance,
miss," he said. "And your sister?" He reached out toward
Nancy, but she turned her face farther to the wall and
kept pushing the darning needle.

"She's feelin' poorly," Becky said in a slight voice.

"I hope it's nothing serious." Finally the colonel
seemed to be at a loss for more words and took one more
glance around the room. "Thank you again for your gen-
erosity, ma'am, ladies," he nodded and then putting his
hat back on, said, "Men," and motioned the other two
out the door.

"Warn't nothin' to be afeared of," Granny said as
she stood by the window watching them throw the sacks
of vegetables over the back of the mule which trailed

behind their horses. Nancy said nothing, but cautiously rose from the bed and looked out the window to watch them ride away. *I've got to get up to Josh,* she thought, *but not till I'm sure they're gone. It's gettin' too danger-ous 'round here. Josh'll have to ride soon, healed or not.*

Becky and Nancy went back outside to their corn crushing. "Don't you want to run up and tell Josh 'bout what happened?" Becky asked, but Nancy cautioned, "Not too soon, Becky. It's important we carry on like ordinary till we're sure they're gone." She picked up the grinding stone and threw herself into the crushing as hard as she could while Becky poured the corn.

Suddenly a shadow fell across them, and Nancy jerked herself around to find the five Federals right behind them. Colonel Starr and the two other men were already dismounting and another rode his horse around between the girls and the cabin. Then, placing his hand on her shoulder, Colonel Starr said, "Well, Nancy, at last we've got you."

"That's not Nancy Hart. You leave her alone!" Becky shouted. As soon as the words were spoken, she realized what she had done. "Oohh," she wailed, clasping her hands across her mouth.

"Please come with me, Miss Hart, and you, too, miss, since harboring the enemy in time of war is a crime."

Becky's wailing continued, but Nancy stood there stoically and calmly, at least to the observer. Inside she was terrified, and her mind was working frantically. *Josh! Josh! I will not turn and look back, but do you see what's happenin' to me? Josh, do you see?*

"What about the old woman, sir?" the other officer asked. "Do we take her, too?"

Colonel Starr looked at the cabin. The door had been closed and bolted again. He considered silently for a mo-ment, then shook his head. "No, captain. She'd be more trouble than she's worth, another cryin' female." He shifted his head toward Becky. "The old woman won't cause harm."

"I won't cause no harm either, sir," Becky said through tears and sobs. "Let me stay with my granny," she pleaded.

"No miss," Colonel Starr said. "I believe we'll take you with us. You'll be treated properly. We'll leave your granny alone, for now," he added as he looked directly at Nancy.

His meaning was clear. The old woman could be used as a threat to obtain further information. *Josh, I hope you're seein' all this and get yourself outa here afore Becky tells all she knows.*

The two young orderlies were on either side of Nancy and Becky, looking ill at ease, as if they didn't know what to do with female prisoners. "Do they walk, sir?" One finally asked, "Do we tie their hands?"

Then the other man, who had not yet spoken and who was not dressed as an officer, but seemed to have a higher rank, spoke up. "Allow the two young ladies to use my horse, sir. I'll ride with Captain Davis."

Becky's wailing was now quieted to sobs, her face still red and tear streaked. She kept looking toward the cabin, but Granny's head was not even to be seen through the windows.

The gentleman who had offered his horse now gave Becky a step up with his hand and then offered the same to Nancy. Without speaking, she avoided his hand and stretched her foot up to the stirrup, then reaching to the saddle, hitched herself up effortlessly behind Becky. "Hush up, Becky," she whispered. "We'll be all right. Jist hush up and stay calm."

Becky mumbled something; then lifting her apron, she wiped her face and blew her nose.

The men, all mounted now, surrounded the two girls, the colonel in the lead, Captain Davis and the gentleman to the right side, one of the orderlies close in on the left holding the reins, and the last leading the mule directly behind.

"Where are you takin' us, Colonel Starr?" Nancy asked in a clear, strong voice.

"To our quarters in Summersville, Miss Hart," was the reply.

Josh, did you hear that? Nancy rode with her back straight and head held high. She was sure Josh's eyes were fixed on her. She released an arm from Becky's waist and lifted her hand as though to smooth her hair, giving a slight waving motion.

They followed the course of the Gauley River, riding along a trail above the gorge until the trail gradually widened into a road and the road became more travelled. Becky was more subdued than Nancy had ever seen her. She had stopped the crying, but every now and then a deep sob would shake her body.

They entered the town of Summersville, the seat of Nicholas County, and Nancy noticed that it was not much different from the town of Spencer with its courthouse in the center, some shops and town buildings and nice proper stone and frame homes of the more prosperous townspeople. Beyond those, smaller homes were spread farther apart and up the surrounding steep hills. Three of the larger buildings had been commandeered by the Federals, and Colonel Starr rode into the yard of a roomy, comfortable looking frame house and dismounted. "Captain, see that these two young women are incarcerated. Use the old jail building," he ordered, and then handing his horse over to another young orderly, he went inside.

Nancy and Becky were taken to a small, dilapidated building. "You can't expect us to stay here," Nancy exclaimed.

"Ugh, it's filthy," Becky added.

"It's the most secure accommodation available at the moment," Captain Davis said, but even his face showed disgust as he looked inside.

"You can't leave us here, Captain," Nancy said again.

The other gentleman who had been riding with Captain Davis looked inside, too, and shook his head. "These ladies must have cots to sleep on and clean blankets at the very least." Then looking at Nancy, he added, "I'll see what I can do, miss."

Nancy nodded. Then the door was closed and locked, and they were left alone.

The floor was dirt, packed hard. In one corner stood a bucket of water and next to that a cracked chamber pot. The walls were of stone, dripping with black mildew. One small window high up on the wall permitted a shaft of light to enter the room. It was the only source of light. When their eyes became accustomed to the dimness, Nancy took account of their chances to escape. "Boost me up to the window, so I can see out," she said to Becky, who stood trembling, her arms wrapped around her middle.

"How can we stay here? We'll jist die, that's all," she said.

"We ain't dead yet, and I ain't about to die. Now boost me up." She pulled Becky toward the window.

Nancy stood shakily on Becky's clasped hands, clutching the bars and peering out. "What do you see?" Becky asked.

When Nancy lowered herself, she motioned Becky to the center of the small room and lowered her voice. "Them bars are so rotted, we could pull them free, but a guard is posted right under the window. And another blue belly is jist on the corner. Add that to the two in front, and we wouldn't get far. Tonight we'll see how many are guardin' us."

"Tonight?" Becky shivered. "I can't abide the thought of tonight with nary a candle nor blanket. Oh Nancy."

"Let me think," Nancy scolded. "Jist let me think."

Hours slipped away, but it was hard to tell how many from the small amount of light which angled into the dingy room. Nancy and Becky huddled close together on the floor opposite the window. Becky had fallen into an exhausted sleep against Nancy's shoulder, but Nancy

remained awake, listening to every sound she could de-
cipher—the clomp, clomp of a single-mounted soldier
riding by, the muffled voices of the guards' occasional
conversation, the rattle of a passing wagon, a loud call
and then raucous laughter, and the pounding of several
horses at a quick pace. Silence, broken only by a tran-
quil bird song of mid-summer, the loud cawing of a crow.
*A crow? Could that be Josh? Could he have trailed us
here?* Nancy dared not answer the crow caw with one
of her own. The guard outside the window would hear
for sure and know it was not a bird.

Approaching footsteps and voices. Then the clang
of keys and the rattle of the lock. Nancy shook Becky
awake and scrambled to her feet. She did not want anyone to see her huddled frightened in a corner.

"What is it?" Becky yawned and stretched, then suddenly realized where she was.

The door opened and bright light streamed in. The
glare was too strong for Nancy to immediately see who
stood there, but she recognized the voice of the gentleman. "Afternoon ladies. Sorry to have left you in such
dismal surroundings for so long."

Becky, rubbing her eyes in an effort to see more
clearly, spoke in a lowered voice. "Are you gonna shoot
us?"

"Hardly that, miss. Marion H. Kerner at your service,
ladies."

"Follow me," the guard, who stood behind him,
spoke.

Kerner bowed slightly and removed his hat in a sweep-
ing motion toward the door. "This way, ladies."

Nancy and Becky walked outside into the sunlight,
the heat, and the fresh air. Another guard, with a rifle on
his shoulder, fell in behind the girls, as Kerner positioned
himself beside Nancy. "I was able to persuade Colonel
Starr that you two ladies could be confined more com-
fortably at our headquarters."

Becky looked all around as she walked. "Are we gonna be sent home soon? My granny's all alone. She can't milk the cows and do all the chores. She's too old."

"I sympathize with your plight, miss, but that's for the colonel to decide."

Nancy walked behind the guard, looking straight ahead, ignoring the curious stares of the townspeople. "Oh dear, oh dear," Becky lamented as she twisted her apron in her hands.

They were taken to the same large frame house the colonel had entered when they arrived in Summersville. There was a wide front porch with a flowering honeysuckle vine shading one end. The sweet, heavy smell was strong in the heat of the late afternoon.

"All the pleasures of home, ladies," Kerner said with a smile as he ushered them inside, followed by the guard.

Nancy and Becky looked around in wonder at the room with its comfortable furniture, thick rug, and even colored pictures on the walls.

"Quite a difference from that dank hovel, isn't it? The previous occupants, who by all accounts were Southern sympathizers, left so quickly before our arrival, there was even fresh bread still warm in the oven. Miss Hart and Miss...I'm sorry I don't know your name, miss," Kerner said to Becky.

"Oh," she said, realizing he was speaking to her, "Uh, Carpenter, I'm Becky Carpenter."

"Miss Carpenter," Kerner repeated, "Colonel Starr would like to speak with you before we take you to your quarters."

"Thank you," Becky stammered. Nancy merely nodded.

Colonel Starr was seated at a large round table in the dining room, a worn book open in front of him and a glass in his hand. More colored pictures were on the wall, one a portrait of a woman hung above the fireplace. "Ladies," he looked up at them, but did not stand. "Mr. Kerner has spoken on your behalf, and since I can find nothing in the manual to require otherwise, you will be confined within this house and always under armed guard. Your sleeping quarters will be on the attic floor, and your door will remain open at all times. According to the manual on prisoners of war, you will be allowed to exercise outside on the premises for one hour each day. You will be fed the same food my men are fed. You will not fraternize with my men. Is that clear?"

Becky, eyes large, asked, "Frat..er..nize? What does that mean?"

Colonel Starr cleared his throat and looked down at the table. A smile played around his mouth. "That means you will not try to make friends with any of the guards, and that my men will treat you properly and with respect. Do you understand now?"

"Yes," Becky whispered.

He stood. "Soldier, see these prisoners to the room on the third floor, and post a guard outside the door." Then looking at the girls again, he said, "Food will be brought to you at six o'clock. Breakfast is at six in the morning. Tomorrow I will question each of you. Good day."

Kerner, who had been sitting in a padded chair, legs crossed, stood and bowed as the girls left the room under guard.

"You shouldn't show such deference to them, Marion," Nancy heard Colonel Starr say. "They're just a pair of ignorant mountain girls."

"More like mountain sprites," she heard the softer voice of Marion reply before she was out of hearing range. Nancy did not know what deference or sprite meant, but she knew it had a kinder meaning than ignorant mountain girls.

Chapter Fifteen

"Becky, when Colonel Starr questions you today, jist remember you can't talk 'bout Josh," Nancy whispered softly. "It don't matter what else you tell 'em 'bout the rangers, cause they're all done now since Captain Conley was kilt. But no matter what, don't tell them 'bout Josh and the cave."

Becky nodded as she watched herself in the looking glass on the wall. She drew a brush through her long shining hair spread over her shoulders and smiled at what she saw. "Nancy, you know I never seen myself this clear before. Mama had a little cracked hand held lookin' glass, but that got burnt when the Federals came through."

"Becky," Nancy interrupted, still speaking softly, but firmly, "did you hear what I said? Say nothin' 'bout Josh."

"I heard you, don't worry none." Becky still smiled at her reflection as she set the brush down and then gathered her hair, twisted it, and held it upswept to see its effect in the mirror.

Nancy shook her head at the uselessness of talking to Becky. She picked up the flowered chamber pot from beneath the bed and walked to the door. "Pardon me, sir," she smiled at the guard. "But I gotta close the door for a little bit. We need some privacy."

The young man cleared his throat, and his cheeks colored. He looked over his shoulder as if he were being watched. Satisfied that the decision was his alone, he replied, "Yes, miss."

Nancy swiftly shut the door and spoke hurriedly to Becky in a low voice. "Becky, listen to me. You ain't done any more than go to help your poor ol' granny. It ain't your fault that your cousin, that's me, is causin' trouble for the family. And most specially, you don't know nothin' 'bout Josh. You jist gotta get back to help your poor ol' granny. That's what you say to Colonel Starr, and that's all you say. He really has to let you go. He ain't got nothin' against you."

"You really think so, Nancy? To tell the truth, I'm gettin' to like it here. They're treatin' us real fine." Becky sighed.

"Remember! You don't know nothin' 'bout Josh, and I'm your cousin." Nancy threw a towel across the chamber pot and placed it on the floor in the corner.

A slight tap sounded on the door. "Miss," the guard said in a low voice.

"I was jist comin'," Nancy smiled as she pulled the door open.

Back over by the window, she caught a glimpse of her own reflection in the mirror behind Becky's and was taken by surprise at the sight of her dark hair, cropped short above her shoulders. It was no longer of a length to plait or twist into a knot on her head. At least it was clean now, thanks to Kerner who had kindly brought them two basins of warm water, soap, and towels first thing in the morning.

"I thought you ladies might like the opportunity to freshen up a bit after your long ride yesterday and your sojourn in that hovel," he had said so politely.

"You're not like the other soldiers, and you don't wear the uniform," Nancy had ventured, hoping to get some information from him.

"You're correct, Miss Hart. I am a military telegraph operator."

When Nancy gave him a blank look, he continued, "A telegrapher, miss. A civilian who can send and receive messages over telegraph wires. I'm sure you've seen those wires up on the poles. Well, we send important messages from one place to another through those little wires." He smiled, satisfied that he had explained to the charming, but ignorant girls how important his job was.

Nancy nodded, "I always wondered what them wires was for," all the while thinking, *I helped cut more of your message wires than you'll ever know 'bout.*

It was clear to Nancy that if they were to get any help at all or glean any information, it would be through Kerner. He was already concerned for their comfort. Perhaps he would look out for their safety, too, or at least speak up on their behalf.

"I ain't used to bein' this idle," Nancy complained by mid-morning. "Not even a quilt to stitch on or cookin' to be done." They were still in their attic room. Becky had continually returned to the mirror to primp, but now it was growing warm, and she lay on the bed, fanning herself. Nancy could not sit still. She paced back and forth between the two small windows, pretending to admire the view. The small corner window, which was near where the guard stood, held an angled view of the town. If she stuck her head out in hopes of catching a cool breeze, she could probably see the courthouse. The back dormered window was better, though hotter. No movement of air drifted in, but she could kneel in front of it and look down on the yard with its privy, the stable, the depleted garden, and the fence and woods beyond. "I wonder when they'll allow us our hour of exercise in the yard," Nancy murmured, wishing she was down in the cool shade or could look inside the stable. That large horse of the colonel's had looked real fine and had reminded her of Pepper, though more powerful.

Footsteps sounded on the narrow steps to the attic
and then Kerner appeared, beads of sweat visible on his
forehead. Nancy rose immediately from the window, and
Becky sat up lazily on the bed and yawned.

"Ladies, I do apologize for this heat. You must be
stifling up here," he said as he took his handkerchief from
his pocket and wiped his brow. "Well, heat does rise, and
you are at the top of this house."

Becky was on her feet by now, dabbing at her forehead. "Couldn't we stay downstairs during the heat of
the day, Mr. Kerner? It is deathly up here."

"I was just coming to escort you down there, Miss
Carpenter. Colonel Starr is ready to interrogate you, one
at a time."

Nancy felt herself stiffen up. It wasn't so much her
own questioning that frightened her as the questioning of
Becky. Would Becky manage to keep her mouth shut about
Josh? After all, it was Becky who, unthinking, had given
her away as Nancy Hart.

"No need to be frightened, ladies," he said, sensing
their tenseness. "You both seem to be quite harmless to
me."

Mr. Kerner led the way down the steps so narrow
and twisting that they all had to turn inward as if de-
scending a ladder. Becky followed, holding her skirt daintily, then Nancy, then the guard with his gun. They
passed through a room with three beds, most likely
occupied by the officers, then into the hall and down
the main stairway.

It was considerably cooler, though, if possible Nancy
felt even hotter, her heart pounding. *I'll jist walk right in
with Becky*, Nancy thought. *If I can stay, I can head her
off if she starts to tell too much.* On the main floor she
stood right behind Becky, their arms touching.

Colonel Starr was at the dining room table again. He
rose this time. "I'll speak to Miss Carpenter first," he said.

"Becky really don't know nothin', sir," Nancy heard
herself saying. "I'm the one you want. Becky's jist my
cousin and gave me a place to stay."

"Miss Hart," the colonel interrupted, "Miss Carpenter can speak for herself. I'll interrogate you afterward." And with that, he took Becky's arm, offered her a seat, and closed the door.

Nancy sat on the wooden settee in the front hallway. She strained to hear the colonel's questions and Becky's responses, but all she could hear was the low murmur of the colonel's voice, then silence. A grandfather clock stood in the hallway. Its ticking was the only sound. The guard outside the front door coughed. Then silence again, except for the buzzing of a pesky fly. Nancy leaned her head back against the wall, closed her eyes and swatted at the persistent fly. The tick, tick, tick of the clock cut through the air, thick with heat.

"Miss Hart," Kerner's voice interrupted Nancy's concentration, and she opened her eyes. "No need for you to wait here. You'll be much more comfortable in the parlour. My keying machine is there. I'd surely like to show it to you."

Reluctantly Nancy stood and followed him with one glance toward the closed door and the low murmur behind it. The parlour had obviously been rearranged in order to accommodate the telegraph machine and a cumbersome wooden desk in the far corner. A clicking noise suddenly came from the machine.

"Excuse me," Kerner said. "A message is just coming in now. Could be of the utmost importance."

The door to the dining room opened, and Becky emerged. "Colonel Starr says we can stay down here and walk about to get a breath of fresh air after he's finished questionin' you." She smiled at Nancy as though she had just come from a social.

Colonel Starr looked up from the table as Nancy entered the room. "Take a seat," he said. The guard closed the door behind her. The colonel unbottoned the top three buttons of his jacket. "You are Nancy Hart?"

"Yes, sir," Nancy replied in a small voice.

"What is your age?"

"Jist turned sixteen," she answered.

"Where is your home?"

"On the farm where you found me." *Say no more'n you need to,* she told herself repeatedly.

"According to Miss Carpenter, you haven't been there for long. Where is your home?"

"I lived on a farm near Flat Fork in Roane County, but my ma and pa went back down to Tazewell."

Colonel Starr dipped his pen in an inkwell and scribbled on a piece of paper. "Are you or have you ever been a member of the outlawed Moccasin Rangers?" He placed his pen carefully beside the paper and folded his hands, watching Nancy closely.

Careful Nancy, careful. He knows the answer already. Maybe he's waitin' for you to lie. "I helped to cook and wash and mend clothes, sir, for some of the folks who held out in the hills, but that's all I done. Some of them folks was burnt out by the Home Guard."

He dipped the pen once more and wrote. "Do you deny that you are the Miss Nancy Hart mentioned in this paper?" He lifted a creased and yellowed sheet from the table and read aloud. "A liberal reward is offered for information leading to the whereabouts and eventual capture of a Miss Nancy Hart, about 16 years of age, black hair, dark eyes, fair complexion, considered to be comely in appearance, and known to be a Rebel guide and spy. She has been reported in the company of known Confederate guerilla, Perry Conley, for whom a death warrant has been posted by the United States government." He paused and laid the paper down. "Do you deny that?"

Nancy shook her head.

"So, if you are this Nancy Hart, you are aware that the notorious Perry Conley was killed in a skirmish on this past June ninth in nearby Braxton County."

Nancy nodded. Unbidden tears welled up, but she would not let them fall. She could not speak.

"We wish you to provide us with the names and locales of the other Moccasin Rangers."

Nancy lowered her head and shook it slowly from
side to side.

"Do you realize the seriousness of your position, Miss
Hart? At the very least you will be sent to the Old Capitol
Prison in Washington, there to remain for the duration of
the war. If you do not cooperate, it is most likely you will
be tried and hung as a spy." Colonel Starr stared at her,
as if trying to determine the effect his words had on her.
"Now, we begin again. Give me the names and locales of
the other rangers **and**," he said with emphasis, "do you
know who was responsible for the murder of a young
Doctor Poole in the town of Spencer and, subsequently,
his father, Colonel Poole?"

Nancy sat mute.

"Miss Hart, I advise you to think very carefully about
your tenuous position and that of your cousin, Miss Carpenter, and your grandmother and her farm. Their fate
lies in your hands. We will speak further on this matter
tomorrow. I advise you to weigh your options carefully."

Nancy rose, feeling numb. She forced herself to walk
from the room, back straight, head high. She wanted to
go back up to the sweltering attic room, just so she could
be alone to let herself think. She had to think, to compose herself, to figure out some way to get herself out of
this. But here was the guard standing in the doorway
with his rifle, and here in the parlour was the ever present
Kerner, entertaining Becky. They were examining the colored pictures on the walls.

Now Kerner noticed Nancy. "Why, Miss Hart, you
do look quite wilted from this oppressive heat, and your
face is pale." He took her by the arm and seated her in
one of the large stuffed chairs. "Let me pour you a cool
glass of lemonade."

Nancy managed a stiff smile. She could feel the bod-
ice of her dress clinging with sweat, and she was so
thirsty, she gulped the entire glass of lemonade without

stopping. It had a tangy sweetness she had never tasted before. She leaned her head back against the chair while Kerner and Becky went on with their conversation. *Think,* she told herself. *Think. He wòn't do no harm to Becky. That talk about Becky and her granny is all bluff. It's me he wants to hang. I can't wait 'round here for them to send me north to prison.*

"Nancy, isn't that lemonade the most delicious drink you ever tasted?" Becky interrupted her thoughts.

Later the two girls walked around the premises of their prison yard under the guard of a young soldier. "I know we ain't supposed to get friendly with you, but I can't jist call you soldier. What name do you go by?" Becky asked. Nancy walked silently beside them as though she had not a care in the world, but all the while she was assessing her surroundings.

"My name is Clayton, miss. My friends call me Clay." He smiled down at Becky.

"Well, you sure are a tall one, ain't you, Clay? Where are you from?"

"My folks got a farm over to Braxton way, miss."

"Then you ain't too far from home, are you?" Becky replied.

Nancy wandered toward the small fenced area to look at the horses, but Becky, bored with the idea of looking at the animals, wanted to continue the conversation.

"Sorry, miss, but you must stay together," Clayton said.

"It's all right, Private. I'll stay with Miss Hart. You go on with Miss Carpenter." It was Kerner. "Are you fond of horses, Miss Hart?" he asked.

"Well, I guess I been ridin' since I been able to stand. So the answer, Mr. Kerner, is yes, if your meanin' is do I admire them? Most especially that big gray with the white splash on his forehead." Nancy pointed toward a horse that stood at least sixteen hands tall, larger than all the other horses in the pen. He munched contentedly on the sweet grass along the fence line.

"Oh, that's Colonel Starr's horse, Pegasus."

"Peg-a-sus? A funny kind of name for such a big horse."

"Pegasus was a horse in a story told long ago in a country called Greece," Kerner began.

Nancy laughed. "Ain't no country named after grease," she said. "Might as well call it pork fat."

"Well, be that as it may," Kerner chuckled. "A magnificent white horse lived there. He was so fast that he grew huge wings out of his sides, and when humans tried to ride him, he threw them off and flew to the heavens where he became a constellation of stars. And if you look in the southeastern sky on a starlit night, you will find him there."

The horse was meandering slowly toward them now. The other horses parted as he approached the fence where Nancy and Kerner stood. "Well, in all my life, I ain't never seen a horse with wings, specially in the sky."

"I'd be honored to point it out to you one evening," Kerner said as he looked directly into Nancy's eyes.

By this time Pegasus was in front of them. His magnificent head bobbed up and down. "Lookin' for an apple or carrot?" Nancy said to him. "Sorry, I ain't got none." Touching his forehead, she rubbed the star-shaped splash of white. Then she ran her hand down his neck to the jaw line and placed her small fist into the cavity between jaw and neck. It was the largest depression on a horse she ever felt. "But I sure could believe that you got wings," she said. *He'd be fast. Faster'n either Lady or Pepper. And they keep a halter on him, even when he ain't saddled, so there'd be somethin' to hang on to.*

A loud crow call pierced the afternoon sounds around them. Nancy, shading her eyes, looked up, expecting to see a large black bird flying above her, but there was none. Two more crow calls sounded in quick succession. Kerner looked skyward also. "No sign of a crow here," he said. "The bird must be in the woods." He nodded his head toward the trees beyond the fence.

A sudden joy swept over Nancy. *Josh!* She threw her head back and answered, "Caw! Caw!" An immediate "caw" came in response.

Kerner burst into laughter. "That's very good," he said.

"Oh, I lived with lots of crows back home," she said. "You get used to the sound."

"Well, I think you told that old bird to be silent. I hear no more bird conversation."

Nancy gave Pegasus one last pat and started to walk toward the house. "This sun is jist too hot without a bonnet for my head," she said, and she smoothed her hand over her dark hair, black as a crow's wing, hoping Josh was close enough to see.

The days passed slowly, lazily, in a wave of heat. The sun scorched down each day with no relief of a passing shower, and each night the heat lay oppressively over the town of Summersville. Nancy and Becky were treated more like guests than prisoners with Kerner and an array of young guards their constant companions. While Becky thrived on the attention, the illustrated publications Kerner brought them, the fine cloth and colored embroidery threads he supplied, Nancy longed for solitude. She dreamt of the cool green shade of woods, an icy splash of water from a mountain stream, riding Lady, and of Josh.

But each morning came the fearful reminder that she was a prisoner. At nine o'clock sharp Nancy was escorted to Colonel Starr at his chair in the dining room. "Miss Hart," he said on the fourth morning, "my patience is wearing thin. I assure you I have no compunction against seeing you hang even though you are a very young woman. You have three more days in which to decide to give us the information we require. Otherwise, you will be passed on to the authorities at the Old Capitol Prison where, I assure you, you will not be treated to the same accomodations as you and your companion are here in Summersville." He had looked truly angry, his face red and his eyes slightly bulging as if his coat were buttoned too tightly, and he might burst.

In the afternoons as they strolled around the yard for exercise, Nancy listened for another crow call, but none came. *Maybe it wasn't Josh after all. Maybe it was only me wishin' him here.* She took every opportunity to talk to Pegasus, to make him familiar with her voice, her scent, her touch. He would even come to her long low whistle from halfway across the yard, and she would reward him with a handful of fresh grass and a whisper in the ear.

On the sixth day, as Nancy and Becky and the ever present Kerner walked around the side of the house, they heard the creaking of a wagon as it rolled into the yard. A farm wagon, pulled by Red with Josh sitting big as life on the seat, stopped by the kitchen door. "Soldier out front said to bring my vegetables and fruit 'round to the kitchen door. Said you could use all you can get," Josh announced to no one in particular as he swung down from the wagon seat.

Nancy had all she could do to keep from running to him. Josh had still not looked directly at her, and Nancy turned away, controlling her own expression. She looked at Becky whose mouth was open as if to speak Josh's name, and Nancy grabbed her by the arm, turning her around to face her. "Those are right good lookin' peaches, ain't they?" she said meaningfully, trying desperately to convey silence to Becky.

Becky's eyes widened, and then suddenly understanding, she nodded, "Mmm, they do look sweet and juicy."

"Why don't you try one, miss?" Josh reached to a wooden crate and took two peaches, handing one to Becky and one to Nancy. "My sister Ruth Ann is fond of them too."

Other soldiers were around the wagon now, unloading the potatoes, turnips, and two crates of peaches. Captain Davis had come out of the house to examine the produce. "I am authorized to give you salt or flour in trade, but no payment in coin. Is that acceptable?"

Josh nodded. Nancy watched him from the side and knew he, too, was doing all he could to keep from looking at her directly. His light hair, except for one lank strand across his forehead, was hidden by his hat. He still moved stiffly, but he was using both arms. His face was pale, though, and strained about his mouth. She wanted to remove his hat and smooth his hair away from his face and feel his arms around her. Instead she took a bite of the ripe peach.

Kerner was speaking now. "You must not be farming around here. We've scoured the countryside nearby for fresh produce to feed the men."

"I got a fair amount of travellin' to get here," Josh replied. Then for the first time, he looked at Nancy. "You put me in mind of my sister, Ruth Ann," he said. "She'd be here today 'cept she's feelin' poorly. She loves the ride o'er the mountains comin' here, specially by the Gauley River and them cliffs and caves. You ever been there, miss?"

Nancy had bitten deeply into the peach in order to calm herself. A trickle of juice ran down the side of her mouth to her chin. Before she could wipe it away, Kerner pulled a white handkerchief from his pocket with a flourish and offered it to Nancy.

"These peaches sure are nice and juicy," Becky chimed in as though she had not a care in the world. Nancy wiped her chin and handed the handkerchief to Becky.

"I think we'd best leave this man to his business, ladies," Kerner said, taking both Nancy and Becky by the arm and gently moving them along. "We'll enjoy more of these peaches later, perhaps in a cobbler with our dinner tonight."

Nancy, frantic to speak to Josh before she was too far away, turned to answer his question. "No, I ain't never seen them cliffs and caves. I'm sure I'd remember if I did." Their eyes met, and a slight wistful smile crossed Josh's lips. He nodded to her and turned to his wagon. It had all happened so quickly, but Nancy was sure she had Josh's message. *He's waitin' for me at that cave by the Gauley. The same place we went after deliverin' the rifles as Billy and Ruth Ann.*

"Yes indeed," Kerner was speaking again. "These peaches arrived at a most auspicious time."

"I swan, Mr. Kerner," Becky said. "I can't understand half of what you say, but it sure does sound fancy when you say it."

"Well, Miss Carpenter, I mean that the officers and I, myself," he made a small mocking bow, "are invited to a small soiree, or to put it more simply, a dance party this evening at the Brock manse nearby. These peaches will make a very nice offering for the hostess."

"Oh, a dance! Can we come along?" Becky asked.

"Well now, you know, Miss Carpenter, if it were up to me..."

Out of the corner of her eye, Nancy could see Josh leaving. *I should be with 'im!* She turned on Becky, her face white with anger. "Don't be ign'rant. We ain't goin' to no dance. We're prisoners, remember?"

"Well, I only thought..."

"No, Becky, you didn't think. You ain't done much thinkin' since we got here."

"Now, ladies," Kerner said, "I'm sure this situation will be clarified as soon as..."

Before he could speak further, another wagon clattered into the yard. This was a tall black wagon, closed in with a door in the back. Gold letters on the side proclaimed TIMOTHY O'MALLEY, AMBROTYPIST. "Whoa," the driver reined in his horse. He was a small man with a bald head that glistened in the afternoon heat, sleeves rolled up, his shirt unbuttoned at the neck. "Afternoon, Timothy O'Malley, photographer at your service," he called out as he scrambled to the ground. "Have you got a drink of water for old Nellie here?" He nodded toward his horse. "And a ladle of water for me would not go astray."

Nancy had never seen a wagon closed up, like a little house on wheels.

"Well, this is very fortuitous, ladies," Kerner said. "I'm sure Colonel Starr will give his permission for the ambrotypist to stay a few days and picture the soldiers so they can send likenesses home to their families. May I prevail upon you to grace the camera and have a likeness made as a memento for me?" He looked directly at Nancy as he asked the question.

Becky was the one to respond, moving from one foot to the other excitedly. "You mean like the pictures in the *Godey's Lady's Book* you gave us to look at? Like that?"

"Yes, like that," Kerner nodded.

"What's in that big black box on wheels?" Nancy asked.

"Why, that's just the photographic equipment," Kerner replied.

"He might could have bodies piled up in there. Don't think I want naught to do with that. Come on, Becky." She took Becky's arm and started for the house, the guard following. "Sides, we got no fittin' dress nor bonnet to be pictured in."

"But Nancy...," Becky protested. She looked over her shoulder at the amused Kerner as Nancy hurried her toward the house.

They were back upstairs in their sweltering room on the attic floor. "I don't know why you don't want us to have our likeness made," Becky pouted. She lay on the bed, a wet cloth on her forehead. The air in the room was humid and hot. Not the slightest breeze stirred through the window.

Nancy sat on a chair, her back to Becky, looking out the open window. "'Cause, it might be a trick, that's why.

Could be that black box on wheels is made to kill us. Could be they stand us up and shoot us."

"Why, Mr. Kerner wouldn't do anything like that, most especially to you," Becky removed the cloth from her head. "Haven't you given notice to how he looks at you?" she asked.

"Hmmph," Nancy responded.

"Oh, and," Becky added as she just remembered Josh's visit, "what do you think about Josh coming in plain as day?" She sat up eagerly, her mood already changed.

Nancy immediately hushed her and pointed toward the open door with Clayton presumably listening below. She whispered, "I think he's jist lettin' us know he's nearby, Becky. But I thank you not to speak his name nor make mention of him." *Oh Josh, dear Josh. None of that fancy talk like Mr. Kerner. I should have knowed you'd be nearby. Always lookin' out for me.*

The heat made them lazy and drowsy, and they both dozed for a short time until the sound of footsteps awoke them. "Miss Hart, Miss Carpenter, might I join you for a moment, please?" Kerner called from the base of the steps.

It took a moment for Nancy to clear her head and remember where she was. "Yes, of course, Mr. Kerner," she called out and shook Becky awake as she stood up and straightened her dress.

He entered carrying a pitcher of water and a dress over each arm. "Ladies, I apologize if I have awakened you. Colonel Starr has agreed to allow your images to be taken by the itinerant ambrotypist we met earlier. Mr. O'Malley is very popular with the soldiers. Why, he's taking the likenesses of the men, one after another. I assure you it is perfectly harmless."

"Well, it is temptin' to go on down inta the yard again and get outa this heat," Nancy replied. Becky smiled hopefully. "But," she continued. Becky's smile faded and her lower lip pushed out into a pout. "As I said afore, we

ain't got no fittin' dresses nor bonnets to wear to have
our likenesses made."

"I have prevailed upon one of our Summersville neighbor ladies to lend two of her dresses." He placed the
pitcher on the washstand beneath the mirror. "Miss Hart,
this blue would be most pleasing with your fair complexion and dark hair."

Nancy saw the beautiful blue taffeta material, yards
and yards of it, and smiled. "Well, I ain't never had nothin'
quite so fine to wear, Mr. Kerner. Thank you."

"You are most welcome, Miss Hart. And Miss Carpenter, this green will complement your eyes." He held
the dress high.

Becky's eyes were wide with delight. "Mr. Kerner,
it's beautiful and looks to be just my size."

"And here is the final touch," Kerner said as he pro-
duced a hat, complete with a feather. "I had to use some
ingenuity, but I believe I've made a passable bonnet." He
handed them the blue soldier's cap, crown flattened and
reshaped with a blue plume hanging smartly down the
side. "I'm afraid my millinery skills permitted me only one
creation, ladies. You will have to share the bonnet." He
bowed. "I'll return in one-half hour to escort you down to
the ambrotypist." He left, shutting the door behind him.

They removed their old, soiled dresses they had worn
steadily since their capture nearly a week before. Nancy
had to admit it felt good to put on a clean dress. Becky
wrinkled her nose and tossed her worn calico dress in the
corner. "We won't wear those again until we can scrub
them clean."

Three small wooden steps were placed at the back
of the ambrotypist's wagon. The door opened and
O'Malley's bald pate, wet with perspiration, stuck out.
"Which of you lovely ladies will be first?" he questioned.

Becky eagerly snatched the styled bonnet from
Nancy's hands and stepped lightly up the wooden steps,

following O'Malley's head inside. The door shut. Nancy gulped as Becky was swallowed up into the dark and mysterious recessses of the "little house." Nancy nervously began to pace. The unfamiliar weight of the yards of taffeta skirt pulled heavily on her. *Blast and blazes, I wish I was back in britches, ridin' Lady through the cool woods!* She kicked at the material of the skirt to get it out of her way and tugged at the sloping neckline which kept slipping off her bare shoulders.

"Sorry, miss, but you can't walk too far away," the guard called to her. He was standing at the steps to the wagon.

"I ain't goin' nowhere," she replied as she turned towards him quickly and nearly tripped over the long skirt.

"Miss Carpenter will soon be finished, and then you can go in," Kerner said to Nancy in an effort to calm her.

"Must be hotter 'n Hades in that little black box," she replied.

"Ahem," Kerner cleared his throat, embarrassed by Nancy's unladylike outburst. "Yes, well, if you prefer, Miss Hart, O'Malley can take your likeness out here. I'm sure it can be arranged."

"Yes, I surely do **prefer**, Mr. Kerner, for I ain't climbin' inta any black box, not for you nor anybody." She turned her back.

"Very well, Miss Hart. I'll see what can be done."

The door swung open and Becky, lifting her skirt daintily above her ankles, backed down the steps. "Oh, Nancy," she said, "it's easy. He just puts a metal holder on the back of your head, explodes a flash of light, and hides under a black cover..." She paused for a breath.

"That's all I need to know 'bout," Nancy said as she started to walk away.

"Stay together, ladies," the guard pleaded as he took off behind Nancy and looked back at Becky.

"But Nancy, it's easy," she said.

"Miss Hart! Miss Hart," Kerner caught up with Nancy. "Really, give me the opportunity to talk with O'Malley, and we'll get him to set up his equipment here in the open...please."

"Well," Nancy replied reluctantly.

A half hour later, with all the trappings set up outside the wagon, Nancy sat on the camp stool while Becky placed the hat on her head and then patted her short hair into place and adjusted her dress just off her shoulders. Mr. O'Malley brought the head stand around behind her. "Now just lean your head into this and it will hold you still."

The feel of the metal grip around the back of her neck was too much. It was like being hung from behind. Nancy jerked her head forward. "I can hold my own head still, or I ain't doin' this."

"All right, all right, miss!" O'Malley was losing his patience. He took the stand away, muttering, "I'll take soldiers over ladies any day. Movin' all my equipment into the bright sunshine...But you must hold completely still for at least fifteen seconds, and don't so much as take a breath or blink your eyes, or you will ruin the image!" He disappeared under the heavy black curtain around the camera. In a few seconds he reappeared. "Move your head just a bit to the right, and hold your breath." He withdrew again.

Nancy sat stiff and straight. She did not move. She did not smile. When he finished, O'Malley told the girls that their likenesses would be ready presently.

"I can't wait!" Becky gushed.

"Let's move to the shade of the porch," Kerner suggested. "Perhaps I can prevail upon the cook to provide a pitcher of lemonade."

Finally O'Malley approached. "Here we are, ladies, and finer portraits I've not seen the like of." He held out the small squares of tin to each of them. As Kerner pulled some bills from his pocket and settled with O'Malley, Nancy stared at her portrait. She saw her own somber face, staring back at her, eyes sorrowful, mouth downturned, and that comical hat. *This ain't me, nor nothin' like me,* she thought. But Becky was dancing around the porch, holding her likeness before her. "It's just like the pictures in the book!" she squealed. Kerner leaned back in his chair and smiled.

Chapter Sixteen

The grandfather clock, two floors below, chimed faintly. Nancy counted one by one. *Twelve. It's midnight, and the party'll be breakin' up soon.* Becky had finally fallen asleep, but Nancy, still wearing the borrowed blue dress, stood by the dormered window. A full moon lit the yard below, and she could see the horses occasionally move about the fenced area outside the barn. Laughter drifted through the open windows of the Brock manse down the cobbled street, and then music began again. *I gotta move now. There won't be another chance like this with all the men outa the house, save the one guard.* She went to the bed and looked at Becky, sound asleep. *Sorry, Becky, I hope you understand. But it's best if you don't know nothin' 'bout what happened. And they won't hurt you none. I'm the one the colonel wants to hang.* She laid her hand briefly on the bed and then slipped out the door and down the steep narrow steps.

The young guard, Clayton, was stationed in the room below. He sat in a chair facing the attic stairs and dozed lightly, his rifle resting on the floor next to him. His head jerked up when he saw Nancy, and he grabbed the gun and stood. "Miss, I thought you were asleep up there."

"Sorry to bother you, Clay," Nancy said, a timid smile on her lips, her heart pounding in her chest. "I couldn't sleep, and I didn't want to wake Becky. Do you mind if I come down to talk a bit? I get so lonesome, and that room is so small and so hot." She lifted her arms up in a wide stretch and then rubbed her back.

The young guard shifted his feet and held his gun awkwardly, not quite knowing what to do. He blushed as he spoke. "I reckon it's all right for you to stay down here for awhile. The officers will be returning soon."

"I been hearin' the music from the party," Nancy said. She was nervous, but she had to keep talking. "It put me in mind of when I was back home. It seems so long ago now. I miss my home and my fam'ly. Don't you?"

Clay nodded and shifted again.

"I used to go huntin', too, with my pa and my brothers, but I ain't never held a rifle as big as yours." She pointed toward his gun, and he moved it to his other hand, not sure if he should hold it against his shoulder or point it down at the floor. "Is it very heavy?" Nancy asked.

"Naw, not for me," Clay answered, becoming more at ease. "But I reckon for you it would feel right heavy."

"Let me feel the heft of it." She smiled as she stepped forward.

"Well now, Miss Nancy, I really shouldn't but I reckon it won't do no harm. Take a caution, it's loaded you know," Clay warned.

"I don't even know if I'd be able to lift it," Nancy laughed. He held out the gun and placed it across her outstretched arms. "Oh my, it surely is heavy." She turned her back and cradled the rifle as she walked away from him across the room. The music from the party down the street ended. In the silence that followed, Nancy asked, "Clay, do I look like a dangerous spy to you?"

"No, Miss Nancy, you surely don't."

"Then why don't you jist let me go?"

"You know I can't do that."

The music began again. The fiddles played "Good Night Ladies." Nancy stiffened. *The last dance.* She lowered the heavy gun against her hip and cradled the barrel with her left hand.

"Good night ladies, we're going to leave you now...," a chorus of men's voices sang.

Nancy swung around to face Clay and pulled the hammer on the side of the gun. Click, click.

"No, don't touch the..." Clay stepped forward, his arm extended.

Nancy pulled the trigger. The sound and the kick of the rifle were overpowering. She managed to stay on her feet as Clay fell to the floor amidst a cloud of gray smoke. Nancy did not look; she did not think; she simply dropped the rifle, picked up her skirt, and ran. Her ears, the whole house, still rang from the deafening noise. She was down the main staircase and out the front door. No one was in sight. Her ears had a strange silent feeling to them. She raced around to the back of the house and across the yard to the barn, giving out a low whistle. Nearly tripping on the folds of her long dress, she climbed up on the fence. Pegasus was there, and suddenly, as if something popped, her ears were clear. She could hear pounding footsteps and men shouting orders. "Pegasus!" she said as she swung herself onto the broad back of the horse. The men were closer now. She could see the forms in the moonlight, racing toward the house. She grasped the halter and the mane of the horse and circled the small corral. The horse gained speed. He seemed to know what was expected of him. "Now, Pegasus, now." Nancy dug her knees into the horse's sides and leaned forward, close to his neck. Pegasus leaped.

For a moment horse and rider were silhouetted against the light of the full moon, between earth and sky. "There she is! There!" "Shoot!" The orders came out of the darkness. A gun fired and another and another. But it was too late. Nancy and Pegasus thundered away from the town of Summersville.

The bright light of the moon showed the way, but at the same time it would be helping the Federals, too. Nancy knew she had to get off the road as soon as she could determine where she was. Her first thought was to get to Josh if she could find him. *Josh, Josh, you gotta be at the Gauley Cave. That's gotta be what you was tellin' me.* She did not allow herself to think of not finding him there.

The road narrowed and entered a wooded area as they neared the river. It was darker under the heavy cover of leaves. Nancy slowed Pegasus and searched frantically for a path leading off the road. Pegasus was breathing heavily and lathered with sweat, and Nancy found it difficult to stay on his wide, slippery back without the aid of a saddle and stirrups. She slowed him further to a walk and crooned gently, "Good boy, Peg, good boy." Then she listened for the sound of voices or other hooves in pursuit. She heard nothing but the night sounds and the still heavy breathing of the horse, or maybe it was her own breathing and heart pounding. A sob escaped her, and for a moment, she had a vision of Clayton lying on the floor amidst the cloud of smoke. She shook her head clear and left the road. "Come on Peg. We gotta find Josh."

There was no trail. They pushed through the thick underbrush always moving toward the sound of the river. Finally they reached a clearing, and Nancy realized she was very close. There was that tree stump and just yonder, past the two boulders, was the steep path that led down to the cave above the rapids. She literally slid off Pegasus' high back, her heavy skirt falling in burdensome folds about her feet. Bunching the skirt up in one arm and grasping the horse's halter with the other, she stepped carefully toward the path. The huge horse snorted and pulled his head up away from her hand, refusing to move forward. "Pegasus," she whispered, and then she heard the distinct click of a musket hammer being pulled back.

She whirled around, and then she saw him. Josh stood in the middle of the trail, legs apart, hair shining silvery in the moonlight, and musket raised against his shoulder, pointing straight at her.

"Josh, it's me...Nan."

Josh barely had time to place the gun on the ground before she was throwing her arms wildly around his neck, nearly knocking him off balance. "Nan, Nan," he said. Then laughing, "Easy, or we'll both be swimmin' in the Gauley."

"Josh, when I seen you drive inta the yard today, I couldn't breathe. I jist wanted to run to you." She rested her head against his chest.

"I couldn't abide another day without you," he whispered. "Were you followed?"

"I don't know, but they shot at me."

"Are you hit?" he gasped, holding her gently away from him.

"No, I was gone a fair piece by the time they got to their guns. But Josh," Nancy's voice broke and she struggled to go on speaking. "I...I shot a guard. I...I had to...It was the only chance I had to get away—"

"Nan," Josh interrupted, gripping her arms tightly.

"No, Josh, listen. This was diff'rent. It warn't like shootin' in a raid or shootin' a varmint like Colonel Poole. It...he...Clay...was right nice...and I jist...kilt him." Sobbing now, she leaned into him, exhausted.

"Nan," Josh held her chin gently, looking straight into her eyes, "this is war. And war means killin' when you have to. You're fightin' for yer own life. You had no choice, Nan. They would have hung you." He pulled her close. "And if they did that, I'd die, too." They stood silently for a few moments. The only sound was of the rushing water below.

"Now we gotta get you to safety. No more hidin' out in the caves or mountains this side of the Federal lines. Word'll be out, and any blue belly that sees you will shoot you quick." Josh hugged her roughly to him again. "We're headin' down to Greenbrier Valley to Gen'ral Patton's troops. And you're stayin' safe till this war's over. Lady's down in the cave with Red. I had a time gettin' them down there."

"Oh, Lady! Thank you, Josh. But what will we do with Pegasus? We can't jist leave him here."

"You said they shot at you, Nan. Let's make 'em think they wounded you. I'll check my trap. If there's an animal, we'll use the blood. Otherwise we'll jist send him back riderless."

Nancy scrambled down the steep path to the cave where the horses were hidden. "Lady," she called. Before she reached the dark opening, she heard a whinnying greeting from the horse. "You didn't forget me, girl, did you?" Lady shook her head up and down. "I know, girl, but we ain't got time to play now."

Quickly Nancy looked around the cave which was dimly lit by an oil lamp in the back corner. There was the quilt Alice had made and her britches and shirt folded neatly on top. She pulled off the fancy blue dress, leaving it in a heap on the stone floor, and donned the familiar britches and shirt. Then retrieving the dress, she emerged from the cave. Walking close to the steep edge of the cliff, she flung it away toward the whirling water below. The yards of taffeta caught the breeze and sailed downward. But it did not sink into the churning river as Nancy intended. Instead it caught on a bramble halfway down and hung there, waving like a dark flag in the bright moonlight.

By the time she reached the trail above, Josh had returned with a rabbit dangling by its ears. Deftly taking his hunting knife, he slit it open from neck to stomach. The animal twitched its hind legs desperately for a few seconds; then it was still. Blood gushed from the open wound. "Stand clear," he warned Nancy as he gripped Pegasus firmly by the halter and smeared the blood from the dead animal down the side of the horses' neck and across the withers. Pegasus gave out a loud snort, pulling free from Josh's grip and rearing up on his haunches, shaking his head at the scent of the fresh blood. Josh stepped back. When Pegasus' front hooves hit the ground again, he was off, into the woods, racing back in the direction they had come.

"No time to waste, Nan. Only a few more hours of dark." Josh flung the rabbit carcass over the cliff to the river below and wiped his hands across his pants. "Let's get Lady and Red saddled and outa here."

It was well into the next day when Nancy and Josh passed the questioning of the first picket and then forded the Greenbrier River at a shallow point. At the far bank, the horses lowered their heads to drink. Smoke rose from small cookfires. The aromas of coffee, wood burning, and other more pungent odors filled the air. The jangle of horses' harnesses, the shouting of men's voices, the sharp rattle of a drum roll, and the plaintive melody of a single harmonica could be heard in welcoming harmony, the safety of the Confederate lines of the 22nd Virginia Infantry. Josh tenderly held Nancy's hand. "We're home, Nan. It's all over now," he said.

"Or all jist beginnin'," Nancy replied.

* * * * *

Nancy, the grandmother now, had finished her story. Her slow, gnarled fingers fumbled with the buttons on Myrtle's nightdress, and then she held the covers open as her granddaughter climbed into bed.

"And you rode back with the Confederate cavalry soldiers a week later and took them blue bellies prisoners," Myrtle said proudly.

"Blazes, I did...didn't I," Nancy spoke more to herself than to the child.

"And then you and Granddaddy Josh was married," Myrtle finished, more softly now through a wide yawn.

Nancy nodded again. "But not for nearly three more long years. The war was still young that summer of eighteen and sixty-two." Her hand trailed across the worn quilt, faded now and ragged along the edges. She could no longer see the fine, small stitching as she traced the circular patterns of the wedding ring quilt. "All that was long ago, child, so long ago," she murmured.

And in her mind, Nancy could see Alice, head bent, stitching away on the quilt; Luke standing in the small cabin, head and shoulders snow covered, smiling as he held out two pheasants, "fer Christmas dinner"; Will seated at the table in the warm kitchen and Mary serving fresh-baked biscuits to the young'uns; the captain, a mountain of a man, fighting to the last like a great, wounded bear; and Josh, dear Josh, coming home after the war, walking through the hollow until he saw her plowing on the hill. She was not sure it was him until he dropped his haversack, musket, and hat. Oh, that cornsilk hair, shining in the sun! How she had skedaddled down the hillside then!

"All so long ago," she repeated to Myrtle. But the child was fast asleep.

Epilogue

At four o'clock in the morning of July 25, 1862, one week after her escape on Lieutenant Colonel Starr's horse, Nancy Hart returned to Summersville at the head of some two hundred Confederate mounted infantry under command of Major R. Augustus Bailey. They overran the pickets outside of town and entered the sleepy streets of Summersville unopposed. Only ten shots were fired; three houses, including the commissary storehouse, were burned; eight mules and twelve horses were confiscated; and Lieutenant Colonel Starr and his men were taken prisoner. Nancy Hart interceded for Marion Kerner, the telegrapher, due to all the kindnesses he showed to her during her captivity. Major Bailey released Kerner, who was promptly recaptured while attempting to relay a telegraph message to the Federal forces at Gauley Bridge. He, along with the others, was sent to Libby Prison in Richmond, Virginia. Paroled before the end of the war, Kerner later told his story of Nancy Hart in the May 26, 1910 issue of *Lesley's Weekly*.

Becky Carpenter returned unharmed to her family. At war's end, she married a Federal officer and settled in the North. Luke and Alice lived out their lives on their small homestead in Calhoun County. Mary Price raised her children in Kentucky. She never remarried.

Joshua Douglas joined Captain George Downs' Company A, 19th Virginia Cavalry, his enlistment antedated to July 15, 1861 in order to protect him from prosecution for acts committed while riding with Perry Conley's Moccasin Rangers. Josh returned safely from the war. They settled at the head of Spring Creek in Greenbrier County, where he built Nancy the large cabin with a chimney at each end, just as he had promised. They raised two sons.

Lady lived to the fine old age of twenty years. She often carried the young Douglas boys around their meadow, just as she had carried Nancy years before.

Pegasus carried his Federal rider safely through many battles, but was killed by Confederate cannonfire at the Battle of Gettysburg.

As for the other war, with its "heap of sadness and grief," which Nancy predicted while viewing the Great Comet of 1910: World War I began in Europe on July 28, 1914; the United States was drawn into the war on April 6, 1917.

Edith Hemingway is a graduate of Spalding University's MFA program, with a concentration in writing for children. When she's not working on a new novel, Ms. Hemingway is teaching creative writing workshops at area community colleges and at Misty Hill Lodge, her secluded 1930s-era log cabin on Braddock Mountain in Maryland. Visit her Web site at www.ediehemingway.com.

Jacqueline Shields has dedicated much of her time to advocacy for the disabled, winning awards and citations along the way. Ms. Shields has written a monthly column "Handicapped Almanac" for the Frederick News Post. Appointed by the governor of Maryland to a state advisory committee on disabilities, she served in that capacity for twelve years.

The authors met in a creative writing class. Inspired by the locale of their homes between Gettysburg and Antietam, they have collaborated on two Civil War novels. *Drums of War* (originally published as *Broken Drum*) and *Rebel Hart* have both been licensed by Scholastic Book Fairs and Book Clubs.

Literature Circle Questions

Use the questions and activities that follow to get more out of the experience of reading *Rebel Hart* by Edith Morris Hemingway and Jacqueline Cosgrove Shields.

1. Most of *Rebel Hart* takes place in western Virginia. In chapter one, what do we learn about the political situation in this area?

2. What is Nancy Hart's first impression of Captain Conley?

3. To avoid detection by Federal troops, what methods do the Moccasin Rangers use for communicating with each other?

4. At the dance in chapter one, Nancy yells out to the passing Federal troops: "Hurrah for Jeff Davis!" Why does she do this? What does this action show about her?

5. Nancy asks her brother-in-law, Will, to tell Captain Conley that she wishes to join the Moccasin Rangers, but Will refuses. Give at least three reasons why Will rejects Nancy's request.

6. Immediately after joining the Rangers, Nancy is disappointed to find that her new situation does not match her expectations. Why is she so frustrated?

7. In chapter two, Nancy finds herself talking to her horse, Jeremiah, about wanting to join the Moccasin Rangers. Why does she say that she wants to join them? Besides what she says out loud, what might be her unspoken reasons for wanting to join Captain Conley's group?

8. Compare *Rebel Hart* with other accounts of the Civil War, such as your history textbook, other novels, or perhaps a movie or documentary you have seen. How does this account differ from others you have read or viewed?

9. Why is Nancy's brother-in-law, Will, killed by the Federal troops? Nancy's father blames her, saying, "You, goin' off with them bushwhackers brought all this down on our heads!" (p. 55). To what extent do you think Nancy is responsible for her brother-in-law's death?

10. What makes Nancy Hart a good spy? What characteristics help her fulfill her missions for the Moccasin Rangers?

11. How does the arrival of Mary's letter in chapter 12 help change Nancy's priorities? From Nancy's response to this letter, what do we learn about how she has changed since the beginning of the novel?

12. The story begins and ends with the elderly Nancy Hart talking with her young granddaughter Myrtle. How does this framing technique affect your reading of the story? Why do you think the authors chose to begin and end Nancy's story this way?

13. When the story begins, Nancy is thrilled at the thought of joining the Moccasin Rangers, but as her involvement with the rebel group grows, her feelings begin to change. Describe how Nancy's thoughts and feelings about the war change over time. What experiences do you think cause these changes?

14. By the end of the novel, Nancy has started learning to read and write with Josh's help. Imagine a letter she might write to her sister, Mary, in Kentucky after the war. Pretend you are Nancy, and write the letter, describing your feelings about the war, your family, Josh, and your experiences with the Moccasin Rangers.

15. To whom would you recommend *Rebel Hart*? Write a specific, detailed recommendation for this person, explaining why you think he or she would enjoy the book.

Note: These questions are keyed to Bloom's Taxonomy as follows: Knowledge: 1–3; Comprehension: 4–6; Application: 7–8; Analysis: 9–10; Synthesis: 11–13; Evaluation: 14–15

Activities

1. Many of the characters in *Rebel Hart* speak in a dialect that reflects the story's setting—western Virginia in the early 1860s. Choose a scene with dialogue to present as a readers' theater to your class. Practice reading your scene expressively to a group of students, and be prepared to present it to the whole class.

2. What do you consider to be the five or six most important scenes from *Rebel Hart*? Create a storyboard in which you illustrate the scenes you think are essential to the novel's plot. For each scene you choose, include a short caption to help explain it, and be prepared to justify why you chose the scenes you did.

3. Imagine that you have been chosen to design a recruitment poster for the Moccasin Rangers. How would you motivate Confederate sympathizers to join your cause? Draw a poster to encourage young people to join Captain Conley's group, using your knowledge of the Moccasin Rangers from *Rebel Hart*.

Also by These Authors:

Drums of War (originally published as *Broken Drum*)